PRAISE F
THE JANE JOURNALS

"A completely charming, cleverly written combination of all Austen's finest works. I was drawn in from the beginning, absolutely enamored with the concept of this series. Doxey's portrayal of Austen characters as students in a modern-day prep school is equal parts hilarious, accurate, and touching. I was captivated from the first page, and I'm anxiously looking forward to the next installment! Doxey's debut fictional series is destined to be a smashing success with the young adult crowd."

—LAUREN WINDER FARNSWORTH, author of *Keeping Kate*

"It is a truth universally acknowledged that a girl in possession of good taste is always in search of a new Jane Austen adaptation. *The Jane Journals* is a fun medley of diary entries, composed by various Austen characters in modern situations. You'll enjoy seeing your favorite stories with a current twist that will have you wondering if *Pride and Prejudice* or *Persuasion* could happen in your neighborhood. Be prepared to be left wanting more!"

— AUBREY MACE, author of *Before the Clock Strikes 30*

"Doxey delivers! *The Jane Journals* had me snickering through each hilarious entry. I don't see myself reading a lot of Jane Austen, but I would read another Doxey, for sure!"

—FRANK L. COLE, author of the Hashbrown Winters series and Guardians series

"Cleverly crafted, wonderfully written, and immensely intriguing—this modern twist on several beloved classics is a must-read for Austen fans or anyone who loves a good romantic comedy."

—KIMIKO CHRISTENSEN HAMMARI, children's book author and editor

"Reading Heidi Doxey's *The Jane Journals* is kind of like getting a peek inside your best friends' diaries. I was hooked from the very first entry. And the more I read, the more I wanted to know about Doxey's delightful diarists—and just how, where, and when their lives would intertwine.

"The wink at Jane Austen, with the spunky voice of main character Elizabeth 'Lizzie' Bennet and her delicious disdain for one Liam 'Darcy' will appeal to Janeites of all ages.

"At turns funny and fanciful, poignant and powerful, Doxey's *Journals* captures the emotion of first loves and first losses in way that will leave readers eager to turn the pages. Honest, original, and completely spot-on, you will love Ms. Eliot for forcing the truth out of every single one of these characters!

"Dear Diary, I am officially in love with this book!"

—ELODIA STRAIN, author of *The Icing on the Cake*

THE **Jane Journals** OF **Pemberley Prep**

HEIDI JO DOXEY

SWEETWATER
BOOKS
AN IMPRINT OF CEDAR FORT, INC.
SPRINGVILLE, UTAH

This is a work of fiction. The characters, names, incidents, places, and dialogue are products of the author's imagination and are not to be construed as real. The opinions and views expressed herein belong solely to the author and do not necessarily represent the opinions or views of Cedar Fort, Inc. Permission for the use of sources, graphics, and photos is also solely the responsibility of the author.

ISBN 13: 978-1-4621-1682-9

Published by Sweetwater Books, an imprint of Cedar Fort, Inc.
2373 W. 700 S., Springville, UT 84663
Distributed by Cedar Fort, Inc., www.cedarfort.com

LIBRARY OF CONGRESS CATALOGING-IN-PUBLICATION DATA

Doxey, Heidi, author.
The Jane journals at Pemberley Prep : Liam Darcy, I loathe you / Heidi Jo Doxey.
pages cm
Based on Jane Austen's favorite stories (Pride and Prejudice, Mansfield Park, Persuasion, Emma, Northanger Abbey), several high school girls have been given an English assignment to keep journal entries about their lives throughout a school year that promises comedy, drama, and cute boys.
ISBN 978-1-4621-1682-9 (perfect bound : alk. paper)
[1. High schools--Fiction. 2. Schools--Fiction. 3. Diaries--Fiction. 4. Love--Fiction.] I. Title. II. Title: Liam Darcy, I loathe you.
PZ7.1.D689Jan 2015
[Fic]--dc23
2014045717

Cover design by Michelle May
Cover design © 2015 by Lyle Mortimer
Edited and typeset by Melissa J. Caldwell

Printed in the United States of America

10 9 8 7 6 5 4 3 2 1

Printed on acid-free paper

to Jenny, Alecia, Kaeli, and Ali—
all Janes and not Lydias
(or Marys, thank goodness)

YEAR

Niall Brandon | Jay Collins | Jack Crawford | Liam Darcy

Peter Feng | Amar Kulkarni | Ravi Mitchell | Philip Elton

Edmund Norris | Henry Tilney | Alex Wickham | Austen Willoughby

BOOK

Lizzie Bennet

Caroline Bingley

Mary Crawford

Alice Du

Vivian Du

Charlotte Lucas

Cate Moreland

Mariah Norris

Priyam Patel

Fiona Price-Bertram

Nila Suresh

Eleanor Tilney

ONE

MONDAY, 8/29

9:00 a.m.

Lizzie

I knew this would happen to me someday.

I got one of those cliché journaling assignments for English. Sorry, Ms. Elliot, if you're reading this. No offense, but it is a cliché. Also, I want to warn you right now that this is the last time I'm going to apologize for anything I write in here. You said you wouldn't read these unless we give you permission—just skim to make sure we're actually writing something—so I figure if I happen to write anything else that offends you, and you happen to read it while you're skimming, that's your problem.

Okay. Introductions.

My name is Elizabeth Bennet. I go by Lizzie, and when I was little my family called me Eliza. Sometimes they still do.

I live in Kensington, which is a tiny little town—more like a neighborhood, really—in the hills above Oakland, California. At the moment, I'm out for a walk on one of my favorite trails. Through the eucalyptus trees and bushes and stuff, you can catch an occasional glimpse of the San Francisco skyline.

I've never been to San Francisco. Isn't that strange?

My dad detests big cities so he's never taken us there. And even though my mom complains loudly about all of the amazing culture we're missing, she hates driving in the city and thinks BART is filthy, so she won't let us ride it. According to her, we'll almost certainly get pulled onto the tracks or we'll get lost and attacked in downtown Oakland or the train will malfunction while we're in the tunnel beneath the Bay. Her best-case scenario is that some drunk pukes on us all. Charlotte, my best friend, has been on BART plenty of times, and she says it's not that bad, but for the sake of my mother's nerves, we avoid public transportation in my family.

Oh well. I'm sure I'll go to San Francisco sometime. I definitely don't plan on staying in Kensington my whole life.

I just started my junior year of high school at Pemberley Prep. It's a private school for girls. Although in my opinion, the fact that it's right next door to Donwell High, which is a private high school for boys, kind of kills the whole "privacy" concept. Yeah . . .

I have four sisters. Four. I know.

Jane, the oldest—and by far most amazing one of us all—just left to start college. Well, I guess "left" is a strong word. Mansfield University is less than an hour away, half an hour without traffic.

Jane theoretically lives on campus. I helped her move

her stuff in myself. But school started a week ago and Jane has yet to spend a night in her dorm. I think she's afraid our family will fall apart without her. She might be right, actually. We have lots of distinct personalities under one roof, and Jane tends to hold us all together.

To be honest, I don't know why my parents ever got married in the first place. They're as opposite as two people can be while still belonging to the same species. I've always gotten along way better with my dad than my mom, and the whole family knows it. My dad is awesome. We both love reading Ernest Hemingway and Ayn Rand, and we like watching Christopher Nolan movies. Stuff that makes you think, but not too much.

My dad works from home as a consultant and spends a lot of time in his office. My mom hates how he never wants to go anywhere, but it's just because he's so busy with his research.

I've never been entirely clear on what my dad is researching, but his library is filled with everything from ancient philosophy to astrophysics. And he lets me borrow anything I want so long as I promise not to read in the kitchen. He has this thing about books getting too close to food. And the oven. And the sink. Anyway, it's great. There's a lot of his books, like Plato and Virgil, that I don't understand, but I've learned a ton from them. I got really into Charles Dickens over the summer. And last Christmas, we read *Les Misérables* together. I love how my dad is always pushing me to think more critically about what I'm reading. And I admire his dedication to learning.

The only thing my mom is dedicated to is making sure we all get married. Preferably to rich men. The kind who will want to pay for elaborate weddings. It would be funny if it weren't so alarming. I mean, no wonder Lydia and Kitty are boy-crazy. They're not even in high school yet, and already they're poring over my mom's bridal magazines and talking about DJs and floral arrangements and videographers.

My mom technically works from home too, as a wedding planner. But she's only planned four weddings in the past six years, so I'm not sure that really counts as working. Mostly she likes to read her magazines, create new wedding boards on Pinterest, and watch those reality shows about girls tackling each other over their dream dresses.

As you might have guessed, Kitty and Lydia are my two youngest sisters. They're complete clones of each other, except that Lydia pretty much thinks for them both. And by "thinks" I mean "flirts." Because Lydia does absolutely no thinking unless it's about how to dump her old boyfriend before her new one finds out about him.

Mary, my middle sister, is a freshman at Pemberley this year and she thinks she knows everything. I can't even tell you how annoying this is. Especially when she's actually right. Also, I'm just gonna say it, Mary has zero social skills. The only friends she has are online ones. I really wish I were making that up, but it's totally true.

So . . . that's my family.

If I were Jane, I would've moved directly out of the house, passed go, and not looked back. Now I'm just biding my time until it's my turn to go to college. And I'm not planning on going to Mansfield University, even if it is one of the best schools in the nation. I need to get away from here. I've got two years left of high school and then I want to see the world. Of course, I'm planning to go to college too, but I also want to wander around Europe and write. Yes, I know that sounds cliché. But it would still be awesome. And after that I want to climb the Andes and sail the Indian Ocean. I want to record the oral histories of nomadic people in Mongolia. I want to join the Peace Corps.

And I definitely do NOT want to see or speak to or hear about Liam Darcy ever, ever, ever again.

3:30 p.m.

♥ Nila ♥

Dear Taylor,

Oh my gosh, girly! I miss you so, so, so much! I can't believe you've already been gone a week!

Did I tell you what happened the day you left? Amar came over that night, asking which one of us cried the most when you set off for the airport. Can you believe him? He is so insensitive.

Nothing is the same without you here. And this would've been our freshman year too! So sad. Now I have to do all this high school stuff without my best friend in the whole world.

Okay, I'm going to stop complaining because I really am happy for you. I can't imagine how

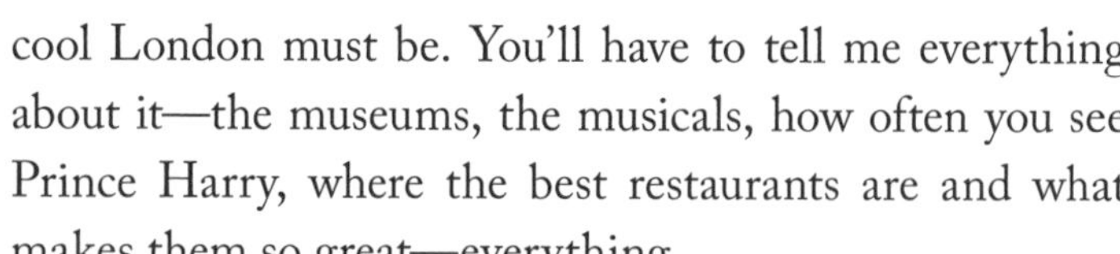

cool London must be. You'll have to tell me everything about it—the museums, the musicals, how often you see Prince Harry, where the best restaurants are and what makes them so great—everything.

Things here are fine. Just normal.

Oh, I guess I should explain a little bit about this letter thing. My English teacher is making us record our lives by writing journals as like an experiment or something. She said we can write whatever we want just as long as we keep writing consistently. So I figured if she's not going to read it, I can turn my journal into letters to you. And that way, by the end of the year, I'll have a little record for you of everything that happened here after you left.

It won't make up for having you so far away, but I think it will help. Of course, I can't actually send you these letters until the end of the school year because they're part of an assignment. That means we'll still need to text and message each other all the time to keep up with everything that happens. But I think this letter thing will still be fun. Or at least it will be fun for me. Haha. Besides, I'd much rather talk to you than to a diary or something.

So today was the first day of school. And like always, some good stuff happened and some bad stuff happened.

Good:

- Amar gave me a ride to and from school so I didn't have to walk.
- My bio teacher is SUPER hot.
- I don't have French with Jane Fairfax this year because she's going to Maple Grove High instead of Pemberley Prep. Yes!

- I think I made a new friend. The girl that sits behind me in bio is named Priyam, and she seemed a little lost, so I talked to her for a bit. Nice girl.

Bad:

- I already have tons of homework.
- My dad had his traditional first-day-of-school freak-out and wouldn't let me leave the house without a scarf and coat, even though by the middle of the day it was ninety-five degrees outside. So then I had to carry that stuff around with me all day.
- Amar keeps pestering me to join Indian club. As far as I can tell, all they do is sit around, play chess, and plan "fun" parties. I like parties, obviously, but with this crowd . . . Well . . . But Amar was like, "You have to come. Anjali helped found Indian club when she was at Pemberley." Of course she did. My sister is a genius and loves chess. But we all know I am nothing like Anjali.
- You weren't at school with me. Boo.

Well, that's a depressing thought to end my first letter with, but I really do have tons of homework and as much as I would love to keep writing to you all the time, I should get back to work. I hope you're taking lots of awesome pictures that you're about to post online so I can see them. And I hope you have a good first day of school too.

Love your bestest best friend forever,

Nila

4:00 p.m.

Cate

Where should I start? I've never written a journal before.

Okay. Here's a little bit about me:

My name is Cate Morland. Catherine, actually. But I go by Cate. I am obsessed with books, especially paranormal stuff and vampires. Except I'm not really into *Twilight*. Too much hype, not enough character development. If I didn't have to go to school and do homework and all that, I would read all day, every day. Actually, that's kind of what I have been doing my whole life up until now.

I used to live with my family in a tiny little town in Idaho in the middle of nowhere. The public school there was kind of a joke. So my mom, who is really well educated, kept all of us at home and homeschooled us. I know some people think homeschooling is weird, but it worked out great for me. I hate school work, so I would do all my lessons as fast as possible to get them over with and then I got to spend the rest of the day reading on our front porch or going exploring in the fields or playing football and capture the flag with my brothers. It was wonderful. I love being outside.

But then one day my mom announced that she wanted me to apply for this scholarship to a private school in California, just to see if I would get it. (Mom has always been a little bit worried that we wouldn't be able to keep up with kids from a regular school.) And when I got the scholarship, my parents talked about it and decided I should actually go.

At first I really hated the idea of leaving my family and moving to a big city where I didn't know anyone. Not that this is even a big city; Kensington is barely big enough to be called its own town. But all of the houses are really close together and it just feels like a city to me compared to where I used to live.

Then my mom pointed out that my brother James would only be half an hour away. He's a sophomore this year at Mansfield University. Also, my scholarship only lasts for a year, so even if it's terrible here at Pemberley Prep, it won't be permanent.

But what really convinced me to come is that when I thought about it more, I realized that as much as I love my family and my old life, nothing was ever going to happen to me there. I mean, I read all these books about these girls who visit incredible places and they fall in love and then usually they find out their boyfriends are actually time thieves or shadow hunters or something. I'm not expecting that part to happen, of course. But I guess I just wanted to try something new and see if I could have my own adventure.

Now that I'm here, though, I feel a lot less adventurous. I got so freaked out the first day or two after my dad dropped me off that I couldn't eat or sleep or do anything really. But that's going away now and I'm starting to settle in.

I live with Mr. and Mrs. Allen, who used to be our neighbors back in Idaho before they moved here.

They don't have any kids and they're excited to have me around to liven things up a bit. Or at least that's what Mr. Allen told me.

Mrs. Allen is really into fashion. She keeps talking about taking me into San Francisco to go shopping, except the way she says it you would think we're going to Mecca instead of the mall. I hope she doesn't expect me to dress like her. My sense of style is pretty much limited to making sure my T-shirt doesn't have any holes in it and that my socks are the same color.

All right, I know I'll have more to write later, but right now I really want to finish my book before dinner.

4:30 p.m.

Anne

Well, it's been an interesting first day. I assigned my students a year-long journaling exercise to improve their writing skills, and I told them that I would keep a journal as well.

I haven't written in a journal since high school, but I think it will be good for me to do it again. Of course, I don't expect to have much to write about; my life is pretty routine. Still, I can't complain. I have a good job. I love my work. Teaching English at my old high school is not what I had planned for myself, but in hindsight it's turned out to be exactly what I needed. It's given my life a sense of purpose that I never had before.

Outside of work, I don't do much. I grew up in this area and I've never left, so you'd think I would have lots of friends around. Sadly, that's not the case. Most of my old friends have either moved away or married and become too busy with their own lives to keep in touch. I do spend time with my younger sister and her family. They still live in the area. Her name is Mary. She and her husband, Charles, have two boys: Charlie and Walter.

My dad and older sister live in Malibu. I spent a month with them there this summer. I think my dad really likes it there, which is good because it was a struggle to get him to even consider moving. But Mrs. Russell and I knew it was the best option. With the amount he spends on clothes and restaurants, there was no way my dad would've been able to keep paying the mortgage on the massive house I grew up in. I wanted him to move somewhere close by, but Mrs. Russell knew it would be easier for him to downsize if he could do it in a new place.

Anyway, it was nice in Malibu. Not really my scene, but the weather was good.

Well, I would write more, but Mary called me on my lunch break to see if I could come watch her kids tonight. She's not feeling well. Again. I love Mary, but I have to admit, she is lucky her boys are so cute. Otherwise I would never have let myself become their default babysitter every time Mary comes down with a cold.

Okay, I have to run. Looking forward to an interesting year!

—A.E.

7:00 p.m.

Vivian

Dear Diary,

Today was the first time my dad wasn't there to take pictures on my first day of school. It has been almost a year since he died. I wish I could tell you how heartbroken I still am. It hits me sometimes at the most unexpected moments, and I just have to stop whatever I'm doing and feel the grief—let it wash over me and consume me.

He was the most loving father, the most tender man. I know nothing will ever be the same anymore. My mother is not the same. She never will be. My parents were so in love. I can only hope that someday, somehow, I will be able to find someone with whom I can share that kind of love.

But I think I'm doomed to live out my life surrounded by people who only pretend to care. No one seems to feel things the way I do.

My sister, Alice, for example. She was so busy trying to coordinate our morning schedule today, that she didn't even remember to take any pictures. And by the time I thought of it, my mom had already left for work.

So I had to console myself with a lame first-day selfie.

If only my dad were still alive. He always remembered to take our pictures on the first day. And he never would've let us move into this teeny tiny apartment.

This is all Alice's fault. She's the one who made us move across town and made my mom get a job. I know she thinks she's helping, but sometimes she just makes it all worse.

Oh well. Maybe tomorrow will be better, but I doubt it.

Yours in misery,
Vivian Du

PS—On the bright side, I loved my first day at Pemberley! It's such a beautiful school. And I really like my English teacher. Ms. Elliot seems to have the soul of a poet. I'm sure we'll get along beautifully.

TWO

TUESDAY, 8/30

10:00 a.m.

FIONA

Ugh.

I am having the worst day ever. I woke up an hour before my alarm was supposed to go off and I couldn't get back to sleep. I hate that. Then, when I wanted to take a shower, it was freezing because Julia, Mariah, and Edmund had all showered before me and used up the hot water.

I was late getting ready, so Edmund had to leave without me. He offered to stay and drive me, but I didn't want him to be late. I know how important his before-school business club meetings are to him. So instead I had to get a ride with my stepmom, Mrs. Norris. She is awful. I know that's rude, or whatever, but it's so true.

The whole time we were in the car, I had to listen to her complain about the school budget. She's, like, obsessed with saving money—doesn't matter if it's at home or at school, where she's the vice principal. I think she's hoping the school board will give her a raise if she can manage not to spend a single penny more than she has to. Or

maybe she's just planning to keep the extra money in the budget for herself.

No. That was a terrible thing to say—something Mary Crawford would say. Mary bugs me. She's always trying to be nice to me, but you can tell she doesn't really mean it. I'm sure she and her brother are hiding something. I don't trust either one of them.

I can't believe Edmund has a crush on Mary. That's what Mariah said at dinner last night. And he didn't deny it.

2:00 p.m.

Lizzie

You would think that with all the excess estrogen in my house, I'd revolt and become a total tomboy. But I actually hate sports and jocks. My best friend, Charlotte, loves to tease me about this. And lately her teasing revolves around this one guy—Wickham.

This brings me to another point. Why do all the guys around here call each other by their last names? It's weird, right? I mean, it's never "Hey, what's up, Jack?" or "How's it going, Sam?" Everything's Elton this, Willoughby that. This makes it extra confusing when you get a couple of brothers who both go by the same name. Like the Tilneys or the Kulkarnis. Whatever.

I mean, it's not like all of us girls go by Bennet. That would be complete chaos.

Back on the subject of jocks—they're the literal worst. They think they know everything. They act like you're so lucky to be seen in their presence, like you should worship them. And so many girls do worship them. It's pathetic. Liam Darcy is the worst of all. He's the captain of the Donwell soccer team and he's completely full of himself. He makes me sick.

But I suppose I shouldn't judge all jocks the same. Wickham, for example, seems like he might actually be a decent human being, even if he does play basketball. I know that technically makes him a jock, but he doesn't act like one at all. And okay, not that I really care that much, but he kind of looks like James Franco in *Freaks & Geeks*, which Charlotte made me binge watch with her on Netflix over the summer. Charlotte is obsessed with that show.

Anyway, Wickham's got an amazing body and when he smiles . . . uh . . . yeah. So obviously I'm attracted to him. And Charlotte thinks he likes me.

We met him once or twice around town over the summer. He just moved to Kensington and started going to Donwell this year. Anyway, he's really funny and charming and good at flirting.

I don't know. I've never really had a guy like me before. I know that's totally pathetic, but anyway, Wickham texted me today just to say he missed me. Isn't that cute? Do you think it means anything?

I know I'm being ridiculous, but I can't help it. He is so hot! I'm sure he's not planning to ask me out or whatever it is that guys do when they like a girl, but who knows? It could happen, right?

3:00 p.m.

ALICE-

Right. So this is supposed to be a journal, but I am so busy right now. The school year just started and there's a ton of stuff going on. We've got the back-to-school dance coming up in less than a month, I have a mile-long to-do list, plus hours of homework already, and I really don't have time to talk about my feelings or my whole life history.

Here's the short version: my name is Alice Du. I'm the oldest of three girls. My dad died last October, so over the summer we moved out of the big house we'd been living in our whole lives and into a much more affordable apartment across town. I'm a lot more practical than the rest of my family. Especially my sister Vivian. We're pretty much opposites, in fact. But I still love her.

I'm the student body president at Pemberley Preparatory. I'm also vice president of the Asian student union, which includes students from Pemberley and Donwell High. And I help run a volunteer tutoring program that's sponsored by the local library. We match at-risk elementary school kids with high school tutor-mentors. This is only our third year of the program, but so far we've had a lot of success.

I'm a senior this year, and I'm planning to attend Mansfield University next year, assuming I get in. I don't want to sound stuck up or anything, but Mansfield is actually my safety school. I'm applying to several other schools to see what my options are. But I'll most likely end up at Mansfield. I like the idea of being able to live at home and help take care of my sisters, and I think I can get a good scholarship at Mansfield, which is the only way I'm going to be able to pay for college.

Anyway, I'm not worried about college admissions. I don't let myself get less than an A in any of my classes and my test scores are much higher than average. Not to mention all this extracurricular stuff I'm involved in.

Speaking of which . . .

To do:

- contact caterers about per-plate estimates for senior ball
- pass out sign-up sheets for tutors in all my classes and see if Vivian will do it in hers
- check with Caroline about the cheerleaders' routine for the two-school rally on Friday (Mrs. Norris doesn't want a repeat of what happened last time they performed in front of the Donwell guys.)
- go over the family budget with Mom
- text Peter?

8:00 p.m.

Cate

Today Mrs. Allen decided to take me shopping with her for some "retail therapy." I don't have a lot of money for new clothes, but Mrs. Allen didn't care about that like I thought she would. In fact, she said that was part of the fun. According to her, the challenge is to get the very best for the very least amount of money.

The nice thing is, Mrs. Allen definitely knows what's in style and what isn't. She gave me lots of helpful tips about how to put together an outfit and she said she'd teach me how to do my hair so it will stop looking so wild. We even bought a straightener for me to use while I'm here and some "product," which apparently means any kind of stuff you put in your hair to make it look the way you want it to.

The last shop we went to wasn't at the mall. It was a little boutique downtown.

The guy working there was so cute! His name is Henry. He is really funny. He kept cracking all these jokes while we were looking around. Mrs. Allen was impressed by how much he knew about clothes. I think he was just trying to be nice to her.

Henry goes to Donwell High, which is the boys' school right next to Pemberley. So maybe I'll see him at the two-school rally on Friday. I hope so. I think he might be the coolest guy I've ever talked to.

I still miss my family, but maybe living here won't be so bad after all.

9:00 p.m.

♥ Nila ♥

Dear Taylor,

I think I might try out to be a cheerleader. I could probably make it on the squad, but I don't know if I'd really want to do it. I'm just so bored here without you around to keep me company. I need a new hobby.

Yesterday I was so desperate for something to do that I asked Amar to help me come up with a list of all the best classic books to read, now that I have so much free time on my hands.

So we made a list, and last night I went through my dad's library to find all of the books. They're sitting in my room now. It's a big stack. I tried to read the first one. Then I tried the next one. And the one after that.

No one told me classic literature was so boring.

I hope Amar doesn't ask me how my reading is coming. I might have to lie to him, and I hate lying, especially to Amar.

I think I'll invite Priyam Patel to sleep over this weekend. She's that girl I told you about who sits behind me in bio.

Oh! And speaking of bio, did I tell you about our new teacher? He is really, really, really hot. His name is Mr. Wentworth. I think he's in his thirties, which is old but not like ancient, you know? Still young enough to look like a movie star is my point. Anyway, he looks exactly like that guy on that old-fashioned movie we watched on my laptop that one time you came over and we made a fort and slept in it. What was that movie? *Girl Friday*? I can't remember now. But you know the guy I'm talking about.

Well, I hope you're still loving London. I miss you tons!

Love,

Nila

THREE

WEDNESDAY, 8/31

7:00 a.m.

Anne

I never thought I would be a teacher.

When I was in high school, I dreamed of becoming a nurse. I also wanted to travel, maybe move to a third-world country for a while and do humanitarian work. I was young and idealistic, like every high school girl ever. (Now that I've been teaching them, I'd know.)

Then my mom died of breast cancer when I was a sophomore. It changed my whole life. My dad, who had left most of the parenting up to my mom, suddenly had three teenage girls to deal with. I think he tried to do his best, but . . . he never really got me. My older sister, Elizabeth, has always been his favorite. She's the prettiest of all of us and looks are really important to my dad.

His idea of comforting us after Mom's death was to take us to the mall and let us pick out new outfits for her funeral. All I wanted to do was be alone and grieve, but my dad told me that I needed to be brave and that too much crying would ruin my complexion. I know he was hurting too. I'm sure deep down he loves me and he was trying to be helpful, but when he says things like that, it only makes me resent him more. My mom would've understood.

Anyway, after she died, I became really close with my mom's best friend, Mrs. Russell. She's kind of become a surrogate mother to me. I know she always has my best interests at heart. And she gives great advice—most of the time.

I trust her judgment. It's just that sometimes I wonder if she loves me a little too much. I wonder if she's so afraid I'll get hurt that she doesn't want me to take any risks. Sometimes life is all about the risks you take. Or, in my case, the ones you don't.

That's what I hope these high school girls can figure out. I don't know if what I'm doing as a teacher will make a difference to them. But at the very least, I hope these journals will help them to reflect a little more on themselves—what it is that they really want from life—so that they can go after it.

And there I go again, being idealistic. Maybe I haven't quite grown out of it yet.

—A.E.

5:00 p.m.

FIONA

I hate the beginning of the school year. The weather won't make up its mind if it's going to be hot or cold. So in the morning you get dressed, and it's freezing outside—actually it's always freezing in my room, except in the middle of summer when it's broiling. I live in the attic of our house, which kind of sounds awesome because I get the whole third floor to myself and I don't have to deal with any of my stepsiblings if I don't want to. But the bad part is that because we live in a really old house, there's, like, no insulation in the attic.

My dad keeps saying he'll fix it sometime, but then he gets that tense look on his face, thinking about the money we don't have for that. And it's even worse when my stepmom is in the room. Whenever my dad so much as mentions spending any kind of money on the house or whatever, she sucks her breath in really fast through her teeth. She doesn't say anything about it in the moment, but for weeks after that she won't shut up about our "financial situation." So I always end up telling my dad it's fine and then I trudge back up here and freeze my butt off through another winter. I'm like the Cinderella of this family, except without the fairy godmother. It freaking sucks. If I didn't have Edmund around, I would've run away from home and moved back in with my mom years ago. Edmund's the only person in this family that actually cares about me. Well, except my dad. But my dad's always too busy with work to notice how I'm doing.

Oh, but anyway, I was talking about how at the beginning of the school year you never know what to wear because the weather is so weird. Like yesterday it was so warm but I wore jeans because it was cold in the morning. Then by lunchtime I was all hot and sweaty. It was gross. So then today I wore shorts but it stayed cold the whole day and I was freezing. By the time school was over, I had to run half of the way home just to stay warm. And I was carrying my oboe case the whole way too, and it kept banging against my legs, so now I think I have a bruise on my thigh.

I hate running.

When I got back here I was exhausted, so I sat down on the couch for a minute to catch my breath and then woke up two hours later. Now I'm late starting dinner. (I make dinners for our family because I'm the only one who isn't busy with sports or rehearsals or work in the afternoons. Told you I was Cinderella.)

I'm also late starting my homework, which means I won't be able to ask Edmund to check my work after I'm done, so I'll probably fail algebra and get held back and my stepmom will call me in to her office at school to yell at me.

And this is why I hate the weather at the beginning of the school year.

8:00 p.m.

Vivian

Dear Diary,

I must say, I am astonished at the deplorable lack of school spirit at Pemberley. And I hear Donwell is even worse. I have spent the entire afternoon helping Caroline, Lucy, and a few of the other cheerleaders decorate the gym at Donwell for the two-school rally. Actually, Caroline didn't do much of the work. She's more the supervisory type. The sad thing is, I know no one will even notice that the color scheme for our decorations is a blend of both school's colors.

I don't even know why I'm in leadership except that Alice is Pemberley's student body pres and supposedly my "involvement" will look good on my transcripts for colleges. Assuming I actually survive high school and make it to college.

The worst part is that all this poster-making and banner-hanging has completely murdered my poetic muse.

How am I supposed to write lyrics that will speak to the souls of millions of people and land me a gig in an ultra-awesome indie/folk/pop band if I'm stuck inside, stringing up Christmas lights for hours and hours and hours and hours on end?

My artistic nature is utterly wasted on manual labor.

When I told my mom about it at dinner, she completely agreed with me. But then she said, "Maybe instead of leadership, you should join the writing club."

I love my mother, I really do. But sometimes she wholly fails to understand how deeply I *feel* the things I write. I can't tarnish their sacredness by reading them out loud to the world to ridicule or even to praise. Alas, no one seems to understand.

Plus Mary Bennet is in the writing club. She scares me.

Love from a partially peeved,

Vivian

8:30 p.m.

Cate

I think I made a friend! Her name is Bella Thorpe and she lives down the street from the Allens. She's a senior at Maple Grove High School, which is the public high school in the next town. And you know what's funny? Our brothers are in the same math class at Mansfield.

I texted James right after I met Bella and he was so glad we knew each other. He said the Thorpes are really cool and that he's been over to their house for dinner a couple of times. He went on and on about how great Bella is. I'm glad he likes my friend.

I know she's older than me, but I feel like Bella and I are going to be really close. I already told her about Henry, that cute guy I met at the boutique shop. She's dying to meet him. We're planning to go back to the boutique tomorrow so she can at least catch a glimpse of him. I'm really nervous and totally excited at the same time. I just hope he's working when we go. He is excessively cute!

9:00 p.m.

Lizzie

I hate cheerleaders. I know, I know. That's such a complete cliché that it's not even worth writing about. It's even more cliché than hating jocks. No one wants to hear the story of the poor persecuted nerdy girl who will never fit in with the popular kids because her IQ is greater than her bra size. But that's not my story. Honestly.

I don't hate cheerleaders as a species. Most of them I don't even know. I just hate the ones at my school.

And maybe just one of them in particular.

Okay, fine. The only cheerleader I really actually hate is Caroline Bingley. She and I have been mortal enemies since the moment she kicked over my easel in kindergarten and claimed I'd made her trip and it was an accident. The next day, in retaliation, I pushed her off the top of the slide. That sounds a lot worse than it was. This was the kindergarten playground. The slide was like a foot off the ground. Anyway, I got sent to time-out for violent behavior and Caroline got a lollipop from the school nurse.

That was the moment I realized two things:

1. Violence is not (usually) the answer
2. When it comes to Caroline, proceed with extreme caution

She is absolutely amazing at manipulating adults in any given situation into seeing things her way. She's an evil genius. I'm not sure if she became cheerleading captain because of her dance skills, her lust for power, or the fact that she blackmailed her way into it. Probably all three.

The point is, Caroline hates me and I hate her.

This is how the world has always been. In this world, my life makes sense.

Until now.

Because apparently my dearest, darling sister Jane went out on a date last night. And who did she go with?

Charles Bingley.

Caroline's older brother.

FOUR

THURSDAY, 9/1

7:30 a.m.

Anne

I had no idea he was here.

How did we get an entire week into the school year without my knowing this?!

Okay, journal. This just got real. Forget all my idealistic ramblings. This is real life and it's happening right now. I just ran into Frederick Wentworth—my ex-boyfriend from high school. Just bumped into him in the hallway on my way to an early morning faculty meeting. It's been years since I last saw him. He looks even better than he used to. I don't even know how that's possible. Meanwhile, all I did this morning was shower and put on mascara. No foundation. No lipstick. Didn't even blow-dry my hair. That's the kind of morning it was.

Holy moly. I can't believe he's here. I can't believe he said hello to me. And not only is he here, but he's teaching here. AT MY SCHOOL. This means I'll have to keep seeing him.

I think I need some air. Sadly, I am still stuck in the aforementioned faculty meeting. Do you think anyone would notice if I got up to use the restroom? Do you think *he* would notice? Probably. What if I just passed out? Would that be noticeable?

OH MY GOSH!!!!!!!!!!!!!! I think I'm having an anxiety attack. I can't breathe.

Okay. Here's what happened. I was running late, so I didn't even stop by my classroom. I parked on the other side of the parking lot, over by the science classes, which is closer to the auditorium, where the meeting was being held. I grabbed all my stuff, walked into the science building, turned the corner into the hallway, and there he was. Bam.

I was so shocked, I froze. My mouth fell open, and I almost dropped all of my papers.

He was standing halfway down the hall from me, talking on his cell phone and not really looking in my direction, so thankfully he didn't see my first dumbfounded moment of shock and awe and aagh! I have never been so close to imploding in my entire life.

When he did look up, I think I made some sort of half-smiling grimace expression. He looked just as shocked as I felt.

Keep in mind that we haven't spoken to each other in eight years. Eight years is a LONG time.

Then he regained his composure, walked down the hall to me, stuck out his hand to shake mine, and said, "Hello, Anne. I thought we'd run into each other one of these days."

Just like that. Like it was no big deal.

I'm pretty sure I shook his hand, but I can't remember

doing it. I think I also said something witty and charming like, "Murghflubehfiimmmm."

He kind of looked at me then, like, "Are you okay?" He didn't say it. But he looked it.

So I nodded. A lot. And I may have been smiling in a manic way. Or in a maniacal way. Either way, it was not ideal.

He said, "This is my classroom. I just started teaching biology here."

"Oh. Wow. I had no idea," I said. (At least I used words this time.) Then I said, "I teach English here."

And he said, "Yes, I know."

And then I told him I was running late for a meeting and he said he was going there too—which makes sense since he is also a member of the faculty—and asked if I wanted to walk with him.

Of course I panicked and said, "No, I need to stop by my classroom first," which was obviously a lie because my classroom is completely on the other side of campus and there is no reason I would've been anywhere close to the science classes if I'd been planning to stop by my classroom. But whatever. He believed me.

He said, "Okay. I'll see you there."

And then I walked back out the doors I'd just come through and into the parking lot. I was severely tempted to get in my car and drive away. But, on reflection, I remembered that I am a twenty-eight-year-old professional woman and I don't need to run away from my problems.

Actually, what I realized was that if I did just leave school with no excuse, I might get fired. And then I'd have to go live with my dad and Elizabeth or move in with Mary and Charles and their cute but completely crazy boys.

How am I going to get through the rest of the day? And what in the world is he doing here? Why did he come back???

Crap. The meeting's over. I'll have to continue this later.

—A.E.

11:00 a.m.

Alice-

I'm still busy, but I discovered that if I take the shortcut through Barton Park on my bike ride to and from the library where I hold my tutoring sessions, I can save exactly five minutes in my bike commute as compared to biking on the streets. This is an extra ten minutes in my schedule, and I've decided that ten minutes is exactly the amount of time I'm willing to spend writing in my English journal.

I just skimmed my last entry and realized I was planning to tell you more about my family.

Now that my dad is gone, it's just me, my mom, and my two sisters, Vivian and Amy. Vivian and I go to Pemberley Prep, and Amy goes to Kellynch Primary.

Although, lately I've been thinking we might need to move Amy to the public school at some point. My mom will hate that idea. She wants everything to stay the same as it was before my dad died. But to be perfectly honest, we just can't afford private school tuition for all of us. Most of my dad's retirement fund and life insurance got eaten up by the hospital bills and funeral expenses when he had a heart attack last year, so I've been doing my best to keep us afloat. We already sold our old house and moved into a tiny apartment over the summer. But I'm worried it won't be enough.

There's no point in asking Vivian to change schools. She's a freshman this year and has been looking forward to high school at Pemberley forever. But maybe I could talk Amy into switching. She's only in sixth grade. I'd go to public school too if it would help, but I'm on a partial scholarship at Pemberley, so my tuition is almost free. And I'm school president. I can't just abandon my responsibilities at Pemberley—as much as I would like to sometimes.

I'm not sure if talking about our family finances really counts as telling you about my family, but it's a big part of my life right now. After my dad died, my mom kind of fell apart. Vivian too. I tried to hold us together, but it's been a rough year. I think we're in a good place now. My mom finally found a job a few months ago and now that school has begun, I'm hoping we'll sort of settle into a routine again.

Class is starting. I have to go.

Oh, I completely forgot to tell you about Peter. I'll do it next time.

Lunch

Lizzie

I just can't believe that of all the possible guys she could go out with at Mansfield, Jane had to pick the one guy who happens to be the older brother of my mortal enemy. What's next? Me going out with Darcy? Ha! Not gonna happen.

Not to mention Caroline would literally kill me if I did that. She's had a crush on Darcy since she could talk—maybe even before then.

Huh. You know what I just realized? Going out with Darcy would actually be a really effective way to spite her. Then again, I'd be going out with Liam Darcy. Ew. Definitely not worth it.

Anyway, it's not like I blame Jane for this. She can't help that she's beautiful and sweet and that every man who meets her falls in love with her. No. I blame Charles. Granted, I've never met the guy. But he's Caroline's older brother and Darcy's best friend. He has to be evil.

Of course, Jane says he's amazing and that they had a wonderful time. But Jane says that about every guy she goes out with. Even that creep who wrote her weird poetry and then disappeared after three weeks.

Maybe I should explain how I know Caroline and Darcy all too well and have never met Charles. It's because he went to an athletic boarding school his whole life. Yeah. I didn't even know those existed. This means that not only is Jane dating a Bingley. She's also dating a jock. I hate jocks. I think I already mentioned that.

Charles and Jane met at Mansfield, where

they're in the same physics class. Apparently he asked to borrow her notes and they've been texting ever since. I know it was only one date so far and maybe I'm overreacting a little, but I just found out they're going out again on Saturday, which is the day after tomorrow. This is a disturbing trend. Right?

4:00 p.m.

♥ Nila ♥

Dear Taylor,

I've changed my mind about cheerleading. I saw them practicing their routine for the rally tomorrow and it's really complicated. Plus Caroline, the head cheerleader, is scary-intense. I mean, yikes.

I'll bet Jane Fairfax is trying out for cheerleading at Maple Grove. That sounds like something she would do. I just have to say it again: I'm so glad she's not around anymore. Everyone was always comparing the two of us. And I was getting really tired of her Little Miss Perfection act.

Amar gave me another lecture on our way to school about how I should be nicer to Jane and her aunties just because they used to be our neighbors. He's probably right, but don't you dare tell him I said that.

Hm . . . what else can I tell you about? Oh, Anjali might be doing some kind of study abroad program next semester. Our dad is not happy about that idea. He's worried something will happen to her if she travels too far from home. But she's running out of classes she needs before she graduates and I know she

wants to take a few courses outside her major just for fun. I wish they'd let us choose our own classes at Pemberley. I'd take all art classes. Wouldn't that be awesome?

What's your school like? Do you miss it here? I mean, obviously you miss me, but what else do you miss?

My dad's on one of his weird raw-food, no-sugar diets again, so I've been trying to get Priyam to sneak junk food into the house for me. She's not as good at it as you were, but someone has to do it. You and I both know there's no way I could survive without chocolate.

Hope you're doing great! Love you tons and lots!

Nila

8:00 p.m.

FIONA

Here's what I don't understand about my stepsister Mariah: she has a boyfriend. So why does she feel the need to make out with so many guys who are *not* her boyfriend? I would never do that. If I were lucky enough to find a guy who liked me and I liked him back, even just a little bit, I would be the best girlfriend ever.

I'd make him cookies and hide them in his backpack and I'd text him all the time just to tell him how great he is. And I would be so nice to his parents. I think that's really important in any potential boyfriend/girlfriend. Plus if he needed help with his homework or if he just wanted to talk for hours and hours, I would always be there for him.

That is not at all how Mariah is with Rushworth. Of course, Rushworth is in college and I don't think he wears a backpack, but still. Mariah doesn't even really seem to like him. She just keeps going out with him so he'll take her to all of the college parties she's so desperate to get into. And for some reason, Julia is jealous of their relationship. It's so weird.

It kind of makes me wonder what would happen if Edmund got a girlfriend. Would Julia be jealous of that too? I don't want to think about that. If Edmund had a girlfriend, I'd never see him anymore and my life would completely and totally suck.

The Crawfords came over for dinner again tonight. They're our new across-the-street neighbors. They moved in over the summer and it seems like we've seen them every single day since then. It drives me crazy. Most of the time when they're here, I try to stay out of everyone's way by going up to my room to do homework, but tonight my dad was here and he wanted me to stay in the dining room and talk to our guests. He's big on social niceties like that.

Usually I like it when my dad's home, but I really didn't want to sit there tonight and watch Julia and Mariah fall all over themselves competing for Jack Crawford's attention.

It's obvious to me that he isn't actually interested in either one of them. He just loves messing with them. So he keeps flirting with them both to see what they'll do next.

I think it's disgusting.

FIVE

FRIDAY, 9/2

9:00 a.m.

Anne

It's been twenty-six hours since The Wentworth Sighting and I haven't seen him again. Of course it helps that I basically hid in my classroom all day yesterday. Then this morning I got to school really early, made a mad dash from my car to my room—completely avoiding the science building and not even looking in that direction.

However, all this time spent hiding has been put to good use. It's given me a chance to do some research. Here's what I've found out about Frederick Wentworth. (And, no, I didn't illegally cyber-stalk him. Anyone could've found this info, assuming they know how to Google.)

- He graduated from college five years ago, same as me.
- Up until last year, he was working at a marine biology station on a tiny little island near Haiti. (Too bad he didn't stay there . . .)
- His sister got married. She's Mrs. Croft now. Apparently that's the same Mrs. Croft who's on

the Pemberley board of trustees. When I asked Mrs. Russell, who is also on the board, about Mrs. Croft, she was kind of vague and said that the Crofts seemed like nice people but they're new to the board this year and no one really knows them well.

- He teaches biology here at Pemberley and coaches the boys soccer team at Donwell.
- On his little "About Me" segment in the school newsletter, he listed peanut butter sandwiches as his favorite food.

That's all I've got so far. But I'll add to this list when I can. The key is to know your enemy. Or opponent. Or whatever he is to me now.

All I'm saying is that I don't want to get caught walking into the next faculty meeting empty-handed. Not when the facts could save me.

Anyway, I have to go. Today is Louisa Musgrove's first day working as a classroom aide, and since I basically got her the job, I feel obliged to help her get settled in.

Of course this means I'll need to leave my classroom and brave the wide campus where at any minute I could round the corner and run into a certain someone again. Oh dear. Wish me luck!

—A.E.

Lunch

Cate

It's funny how Bella knows so much about Pemberley, even though she doesn't go to school here.

Last night she explained the popularity class system, as she calls it. Basically, people are popular at Pemberley or Donwell based on three things: money, family connections, and overall attitude.

You can have only one of these things and still be popular, but you'd have to have a lot of it. Like Mary Crawford. Her family is kind of well-connected and it seems like they have a decent amount of money, but what really makes her popular is her attitude. She comes into a room and just takes charge, you know?

If you have a lot of *two* things on the list, you hardly need to have any of the third thing. Like Anne de Bourgh. She's super rich. She lives next door to the Darcys and her mom practically runs the whole city, so she's really well connected. All of this means she can get away with having no attitude or personality whatsoever and still be popular.

Then there are people who have all three things. They're in their own special subset. These are people like Nila Suresh, who I actually really like. She's a nice girl and she doesn't seem to care that she has money and she's popular, which is pretty cool of her. On the other hand, this group also includes people like Caroline Bingley, who seems to scare the crap out of everyone. And who definitely enjoys the fact that she has more money and popularity than most of the people she meets.

Anyway, I don't actually care that much

about this sort of thing. I know I'm not popular and I never will be. That's fine. I just think it's interesting. I've read lots of books that took place in a regular high school—well, regular until it got attacked by demons or something like that—but I've never actually attended one, so I've never experienced this weird class system thing.

I'm so glad I have Bella here to explain this stuff.

5:00 p.m.

Vivian

Dear Diary,

The two-school rally went well. The cheerleaders performed and then Liam Darcy, the captain of the Donwell soccer team, gave a speech about what a great season this is going to be. Liam's pretty cute. But not as cute as the guy I sat next to at the rally!!! Oh my gosh! His name is Willoughby, and he's completely gorgeous. He's a junior. He loves all the same books and movies and TV shows I do. It's amazing. We even like a lot of the same obscure bands—like the Maureens, Chaos Chaos, and Scouting for Girls. I've never met a guy I had so much in common with.

And I am determined not to lose this chance. We are perfect for each other, and I just know this is meant to be. I friended him on Facebook right after the rally and he's already messaged me twice this afternoon.

I told Alice about him at lunch and she was so underwhelmed. She said he seems nice but that I should be a little more cautious since we only met a few hours ago. Alice is always saying things like that. I don't think she's ever done something impulsive in her entire life.

She's had a crush on this guy Peter for, like, three years now and they're still just friends. It's obvious to me and tons of other people that he likes her, but she never does anything to encourage him and so they're just stuck in this weird friendshippy limbo zone.

I am not going to let that happen to me ever—especially not with Willoughby. He's too amazing to be "just friends" with. I have always believed in love at first sight, and I'm so glad it's finally happening to me!! I can't wait to see him again!

Love from a completely ecstatic,

Vivian

7:00 p.m.

Lizzie

Last night we were all sitting at the dinner table when Jane got a text. We have this rule at our house that if you're texting during family dinner, you have to read your conversation out loud for everyone to hear. My dad made up the rule. I think it was supposed to be a kind of punishment, but my sister Lydia has no shame about it and gleefully reads out the ridiculous things her friends text her. Kitty too.

Mary has yet to get a text at dinnertime.

Jane and I rarely text at dinner but when we do, it's almost always about boring things, so it's no big deal.

Except for a couple of nights ago when Wickham texted me during dinner. But luckily I had left my phone in my room, so I wasn't forced to read that out loud in front of everyone.

Thank goodness, because it was a super cute text and I would hate to have Lydia freak out about it. She's been extra touchy about Wickham lately. I think she's jealous. Which is ridiculous because he doesn't even like her. She's way too young for him. He told me so.

I know how Lydia gets, so I've been trying not to mention how much Wickham and I have been texting. It's probably best for everyone if I keep things low-key for now.

Besides, we've all been too busy following the drama of Jane and Charles. And speaking of Jane, this text she got at dinner last night was not boring. And it wasn't even from Charles. It was from Caroline Bingley, and it read,

> Hey Jane! I love that you've been spending so much time with Charles, but I feel like I haven't seen you in ages! Want to come over for some girl time tomorrow night with me and my sister? My brother's going out with his buddies. XO, Caroline

What?! Since when do Jane and Caroline hang out? I was boggled.

But Lydia was like, "OMG, you should totally go! The Bingleys have this amazing house and you can check it out for us and then talk Charles into throwing a party there!"

My mom was not as thrilled. "What's the point of going over to his house when Charles won't even be there? And why is he hanging out with his friends when he could be spending the evening with you, Jane? What did you do wrong?"

Nice, Mom. Real nice.

Anyway, Jane decided to go—for reasons beyond my comprehension. I can only think of a few kinds of torture that would be less painful to me than spending a whole evening alone with Caroline and May Bingley. But whatever. The problem is that Jane's car is in the shop right now so she wanted to borrow my mom's car.

Except my mom was like, "No. I think you should walk there. That way by the time you need to leave, it'll be dark and Charles will probably be back, so he'll have to give you a ride home."

And Jane—sweet, acquiescent little Jane—agreed with my mom.

Seriously? My dad and I gave each other the look—the one we share when we both know we are the only sane people left in the room.

So right at this moment, my poor older sister is literally walking into the clutches of my mortal enemy.

I guess it could be worse. I could be going with her.

9:00 p.m.

♥ Nila ♥

Dear Taylor,

I have decided to get Priyam a boyfriend. Isn't that nice of me?

Actually, you're the one who inspired me to do this. Remember when I had a crush on your cousin Frank a few summers ago and you said I should go out with him? And then you helped me figure out how to talk to him and stuff?

I want to do that with Priyam. She's so sweet and cute, and she deserves to be happy.

Now I just need to find someone who's worth her time.

She actually has a crush on this guy named Ravi Mitchell. He's on a scholarship at Donwell, just like she is at Pemberley. And it's not like there's anything wrong with that—or with him, I guess. But when I met him, he was so . . . normal. And boring. And kind of immature. I don't know, he was just . . . goofy. Needless to say, I was not impressed.

I know Priyam thinks she likes him, but she can do so much better. I just need to find her someone.

Who do you think she'd be good with?

Okay, I'm going to list some options:

- Henry Tilney seems like a good guy. He's a junior. I don't know him that well, but Amar thinks he's cool. Probably because they both have that same sarcastic sense of humor. For some reason, I just can't see that working for Priyam.
- There's this guy named Willoughby that everyone seems to like. He's new at Donwell this year and he's really charming, but I think he might be too much of a flirt.
- Collins is a freshman like us so at least he's the right age, but he's weird. The only reason he's going on this list is that he lives conveniently close to Priyam.

- William Cox seems okay. You remember him, right? He's kind of nerdy. Likes to study a lot.
- Elton. What do you think? I know he can be a bit of a snob, but objectively speaking he's pretty hot and he's a freshman and at least he knows how to have a normal conversation, which is not something that can be said for a lot of high school boys.

I'm thinking Elton might be the best choice. Now I just need to figure out how to get them together! Ooh! This is going to be so much fun! I just wish you were here to enjoy it with me and give me some pointers. You're so good at this sort of thing. Well, since you can't be here, you'll just have to wish me luck from afar!

Love,

Nila

SIX

SATURDAY, 9/3

9:00 a.m.

Cate

I can't figure out where Henry is. I've stopped by the store where he works practically every day since I saw him there and I've never seen him again. Maybe he got fired? Or maybe he's on vacation? It's strange. Whenever I go back, the only person I see is a scary-looking older lady who stares at me the entire time I'm in her shop. I've almost worked up the nerve to ask her about Henry, but she makes me really nervous.

Anyway, today is Saturday and I want to spend the whole day lying in bed reading. I just got to a really good part in my book. One of the girls discovered she can see these invisible creatures called soul-shifters and now they're hunting her, so she has to escape, but her boyfriend can't see them so he thinks she's crazy. And there's this other guy who's invisible too but he's totally hot and . . . Okay. I'm going to stop writing about it and go read about it instead!

10:00 a.m.

FIONA

School rallies are the worst. You pack everyone into a confined space, like an auditorium or a gym, and then you all yell at each other. And somehow it's supposed to get you excited. It's just loud and obnoxious. The only good parts about yesterday's two-school rally were that I didn't have to go to class and I got to sit next to Edmund at school. He saved me a seat, but then Mary Crawford came and sat next to us. That meant Edmund spent most of the time leaning over me to talk to Mary. I really don't know why he likes her. I mean, sure, she's popular and kind of pretty, but she's a gossip and she rarely has anything interesting to say.

She's always trying to get me to do things with her. I think she thinks of me as some sort of social project. Like she's going to single-handedly save me from the despairs of friendless oblivion. I hate that. I may be a loser, but I don't need her constantly pointing it out to me. My step-sisters are already doing a great job of that.

Besides, I don't even want to be popular. All the popular kids are always getting into trouble for their wild parties and reckless behavior or things like that. I would never do that stuff. I'm better than that. I know I am.

I mean, yeah, my life isn't perfect. But it's not like getting a fashion makeover would change any of that. And no one is going to force me to go out and chat with people I don't know. I hate chatting. I am not a chatty person.

Besides, if I wanted a makeover, I could ask Julia or Mariah. They have so many clothes in their closets that they keep giving me things to store in mine. And their makeup collection has crept out of their bathroom and is now threatening to take over the hallway bookshelves.

Furthermore, I would never want to dress like Mary Crawford. She leaves nothing to the imagination, if you know what I mean. I think that she thinks she looks sexy, but really, she looks trashy.

I'm not trying to be rude. It's just the truth.

11:00 a.m.

Anne

Good news. I managed to make it through all of yesterday without seeing Mr. Wentworth, which is how I've decided to refer to him, even to myself. I don't want to slip up in front of my students and accidentally call him Fred or Freddie. The last thing I need is for some teenage matchmakers to discover that we have a history and then take it upon themselves to get us back together.

For one thing, I'm sure he'd be horrified by that idea. And for another, I have a boyfriend. Sort of. Probably. I'm never really sure with Ben, but I think he still thinks that we're dating—even though it's long distance. So it would probably be wrong of me to even consider doing anything with Fred. I mean Mr. Wentworth.

Actually, have I even talked about Ben in this journal yet?

Hmm . . . I just looked back through all my entries to

check, and I haven't mentioned him. I'm not sure what that says about our relationship.

Here's the scoop: Ben Wick is a guy I met in one of my lit. classes in college. When we first met, we realized we had a lot in common so we started dating, but it was never very serious. I think mostly we've stayed together so that we can tell people we aren't single. He's great, though—really sweet and treats me well and all that. It's just that when I'm being brutally honest with myself, which doesn't happen as often as it should, I can't see a future with him. I mean, just because we happened to go through a simultaneous phase of liking Lord Byron and Sir Walter Scott doesn't mean we're really right for each other. Don't get me wrong, he's a nice guy. He's just a little gloomy sometimes.

But for now, I'm okay with our relationship. Especially since I only see him once or twice a year. He got a job with this company in India after he graduated and they're having him work there for a few years before he can transfer back home. I'd love to go off on some crazy adventure like that, but I've always felt like I had to stay here and take care of things at home.

Maybe someday.

Anyway, with the time difference we don't call each other that often, but we try to email fairly frequently. I like it this way. I get all the benefits of not being single without all the hassle of a real, live boyfriend.

My friends and family are fine with it too. Mrs. Russell likes Ben but wishes he were here more often. My sisters are apathetic about the situation. And I'm not sure if my dad knows I'm still dating Ben, but he's never mentioned him except right after they first met. My dad wouldn't stop talking about how Ben's skin was too tan and his eyes were too far apart. But that's just my dad.

I'm so glad it's the weekend. I was turning into a nervous wreck about this Mr. Wentworth situation. I even stayed at school until seven thirty on a Friday just to be sure I wouldn't run into him in the parking lot. At least I know I won't see him until Monday. Maybe not even then if I'm lucky!

—A.E.

4:00 p.m.

Vivian

Dear Diary,

Oh my gosh! You will never believe what happened to me today!

It's so amazing, it's like something straight out of a movie. Okay. I'm going to start at the beginning so you get the full effect.

This morning I woke up super early, like at six, and couldn't get back to sleep. Normally I sleep in as late as I can on Saturdays, but this morning all I could think about was meeting Willoughby at the rally yesterday. I kept imagining the next time I'd see him and how he seemed just as into me as I was into him. I was so happy I couldn't sleep. Eventually I got restless and decided to wake Amy up and take her to the farmers' market.

Amy loves going to the farmers' market on Saturday mornings. She's always begging me or Alice to take her.

When she was younger, our dad used to go with her all the time so my mom could sleep in.

Anyway, Amy was super excited when I told her where we were going. She got dressed really fast while I wrote a note for my mom and Alice so they'd know where we were. And I thought I grabbed my phone, but I actually didn't. I found out later that I accidentally left it at our apartment.

Anyway, Amy and I started walking to the farmers' market. It's a pretty long walk from our new apartment. But we were doing just fine until we got to the park. I don't know if I've mentioned this before, but all of Kensington is basically one really steep hill, so the fastest way through the park is to go straight down a long hill instead of down the winding path.

As soon as we got there, Amy and I started racing down the hill like we always do, but I didn't notice how wet the grass was. I think the sprinklers had just turned off, and our feet were getting soaked. Also the grass was super slippery.

All of a sudden, my ankle twisted underneath me, and I fell. Amy was going so fast that she couldn't stop. But then I looked up and saw Willoughby there. It was the most amazing thing. In fact, I'm sure it was fate. He was walking by at exactly the right moment. And when I fell, he came rushing over to my aid.

He tried to help me stand up at first, but my ankle was really hurting. So then he actually picked me up and carried me the rest of the way down the hill.

I felt like such a klutz. And when I fell, I'd gotten all wet in the grass. I'm sure I looked awful. But Willoughby—my superhero—didn't seem to care about any of that.

Even if I hadn't liked him before, I would've fallen for him right then. I've never had anyone carry me like that before. He was so strong and so confident and sure of what he was doing. I was seriously swooning.

All too soon, we reached the bottom of the hill and he set me down on a bench. Amy was pretty much in awe of him. He tried to check to make sure that my ankle wasn't broken. It wasn't. It was just sprained really badly. I knew I wouldn't be able to walk to the farmers' market. I couldn't even walk home. But Willoughby said we should wait right there and he'd go get his car and drive us home.

I don't know what we would've done without him. He rescued us! I didn't have my phone or anything so Amy and I would've been stuck there.

It was seriously the most amazing moment of my life.

When Willoughby came back with his car, he drove to our apartment and then he carried me from the car and into my living room. I probably could've walked by then, but I wasn't about to tell him that.

By then Alice and my mom were both awake, and they freaked out when they saw me. Willoughby didn't stay, but he did kiss me on my forehead and say that he'd come over later to check on me.

Then as soon as he left, my mom started freaking out about my ankle. She made Amy and me tell her the whole story about three times. And then she wanted to know all about the guy that had rescued me. Of course, I was happy to talk about Willoughby. I could never get tired of talking about him.

And now it's the middle of the afternoon. I've spent the whole day on the couch, watching chick flicks and being spoiled by everyone in my family. And I think Willoughby will probably come by any minute to see how I'm doing.

This is by far the best day ever. The pain in my ankle was so worth it.

Love,
Vivian

5:00 p.m.

Lizzie

So I realize that pretty much all of my entries involve me ranting about the people I hate most, which would seem to indicate that I am a wrathful/vengeful/crazed lunatic who is obsessed with looking on the bad side of things and people.

I'm not. I love a lot of things about my life. I love the weather outside right now: blue skies with a slight breeze. I love the flowers that grow in our backyard and the smell from my dad's herb garden. I even love school sometimes. I like to read and it's fun to see my friends there. And speaking of my friends, today I've decided to write about someone I love a lot: my best friend, Charlotte.

Charlotte is awesome. She's a year older than me, which makes her a senior and I totally don't know what

I'm going to do without her next year. I'm really hoping the only school she gets into is Mansfield because then I'll still get to see her. Although, I'm not actually planning to attend Mansfield myself, so it'd really only be another year we'd get to have together. But maybe the next year she could transfer to wherever I end up going and then we could be roommates and life would be amazing and we could live out our long and happy days together.

I know that all sounds totally selfish, but that's how much I love Charlotte. I just want to hang out with her forever.

She has this hilariously dark sense of humor and yet somehow she's also totally practical. Plus she will straight-up tell you if what you're wearing makes you look like a werewolfish hybrid pig monster. Like, she actually said that to me last week.

Okay. Now that I've focused on positivity for a significant amount of time, I desperately need to rant because really, really bad things are happening.

When Jane went over to the Bingleys last night, they somehow talked her into going to the Darcys' beach house with them in Carmel next weekend. I'm still not sure what Caroline's up to here, but it can't be good. And now Jane's trying to convince me to come too. Ha. It's true that I love the beach, and even more true that I love Jane, but nothing could induce me to spend an entire weekend with Liam Darcy. Nothing.

6:30 p.m.

Alice-

Today has been a whirlwind. First, Vivian fell and sprained her ankle—and got carried home in the arms of some guy named Willoughby she met at the rally yesterday. Now she's all lovesick and dithery.

My mom is making things worse. I think she's actually encouraging Vivian. She thinks this whole thing is so romantic.

Amy's been going back and forth all day between being just as smitten with Willoughby as Vivian and being mad at Viv for not taking her to the farmers' market like she "promised."

By afternoon, all of the boy talk was really getting to me, so I decided to get out of the house and do something productive with my Saturday. I was at the Kensington library dropping off flyers to advertise my tutoring program when Peter walked up behind me. He loves doing that. He's always trying to catch me off guard. It's incredibly annoying.

Anyway, he was there to check out books for a research paper he has to write. He asked if I wanted to stay for a while and study with him. Part of me really wanted to. I've been so busy that it's been forever since I hung out with him. But then again, part of the reason I've made myself so busy is so I wouldn't have time to be tempted to hang out with him.

I wish I didn't know what I do know about him. I've wished that so many times since I found out. I'm not usually the kind of person to yearn for ignorance. I love to have all the facts about something before I make a decision. But just in this one instance, I really, really wish I didn't know that he's secretly—

Nope. I shouldn't even write it down. I promised I wouldn't tell. And I can't risk anyone reading this, even Ms. Elliot.

SEVEN

SUNDAY, 9/4

10:00 a.m.

Cate

Well, yesterday didn't turn out at all like I expected it to. Right after I finished writing that last entry, before I even had time to grab my book and start reading, the doorbell rang, and then Bella ran up into my bedroom.

She was surprised I was still in bed. She said I'd promised to come with her to visit Mansfield University with our brothers. I really don't remember promising anything like that. In fact, I don't even remember talking about it at all, but then Mrs. Allen came in and said I should get out and enjoy the beautiful weather.

So I said okay and Bella went down to wait in the car while I got ready. I thought it was going to be a fun day that all four of us spent together. But by the time I was ready and went down to meet them, James and Bella had already left in his car, so I had to ride there with John Thorpe.

The ride was bad enough. John wouldn't stop talking about his car.

I thought we'd meet up with James and Bella once we got to the campus, but . . . It. Never. Happened.

I got stuck spending the whole day with John, and she spent the whole day with James. At least she had fun. She texted me all day, talking about how awesome everything on campus was. See?

Bella: Don't you just love all these old buildings?

Me: Where are you??? I thought we were meeting at the entrance to the football stadium!

Bella: We saw a footpath through the trees and it led us to this awesome Greek restaurant. Hurry up and get here! The souvlaki is amazing!

Me: Which Greek restaurant? There are three on this street.

Bella: We finished and James said I have to see the view from the clock tower. Sorry! I tried to get him to wait, but he's so impatient.

Me: Okay. We'll meet you at the clock tower. Just stay there until we get there.

Bella: Oh, we're at the library now. James is so hilarious! He keeps sneaking up behind people who are studying and dancing like crazy. LOL!

By the end of the day, I gave up on trying to meet them. It was ridiculous.

I guess I can't get mad at her for having fun, but still(!!!) I had to spend hours and hours with John, who is a nice enough guy, I guess.

Well, no. He's really not. I hate to say that. I mean, he is Bella's brother, after all. But John is really, really full of himself. All he talked about the whole day was his car and how amazing it is and how he got such a good deal on it. I know he's in college and I should be impressed by him, but I just kept zoning out. I couldn't stop thinking about my book and about Henry and how weird it was that I hadn't seen him.

All in all, the day kind of sucked.

Ugh. Now my feet are sore from all that walking around and I just want to spend the whole day in bed.

Oh, and the worst part is what happened when I got home. First Mrs. Allen wanted to know how I liked Mansfield and I had to lie and tell her I'd had a great time because I didn't want her telling Mrs. Thorpe that I hated hanging out with her son. So Mrs. Allen said that was great. And then she goes, "Do you remember that nice young man who works at that boutique downtown? Well, I ran into him and his sister at the mall today. He asked how you were, Cate. Wasn't that nice?"

I'm so mad! I mean, yes, it's great that Henry is still alive and that he's here in town. I'm very relieved about those things. And it's nice that he remembered my existence enough to ask about me.

But I can't believe I missed a chance to see him and to meet his sister!! I probably would've been out shopping with Mrs. Allen if I hadn't been wandering aimlessly around Mansfield with John Thorpe.

The only good thing about today was Mansfield itself. That place is gorgeous. There are trees everywhere; all of these amazing restaurants close to campus; and so many cool, eclectic old houses to see and places to explore. It was like a dream college. Or university, I guess. What's the difference, anyway? I've never really understood.

I would love to go to school there someday. Too bad my family will never be able to afford it. The only reason James is there is because he's a genius and he did really well on his tests and stuff so he got a full scholarship.

I don't know how John got in. He's no genius.

I shouldn't say stuff like that about Bella's brother.

It's true, though.

11:00 a.m.

Anne

Well, Louisa Musgrove may not be the best classroom aide we've ever had at Pemberley, but she is doing a great job with the cheerleaders. She volunteered to be their assistant coach. I guess when you have a big family, coaching kind of comes naturally. Louisa is my brother-in-law's little sister—one of his little sisters. There are ten kids in their family! Charles is the oldest. Then Rick, Henrietta, Louisa, Josh, Miranda, Donna, Stuart, Toby, and Caleb. I think that's the right order.

I can imagine that with lots of younger siblings and cousins and nephews and neighbors running around all the time, you probably learn crowd-management skills at a very young age. I'm supposed to go over to the Musgroves for dinner tonight, but I just found out that Louisa invited

Mr. Wentworth to come too. Apparently he's been really nice to her, helping her get settled in at Pemberley. And now they've become friends. That sounds like him. He was always good at looking out for the people around him.

I just don't know if I even want to go to dinner now. It will be weird to see him again, and in such a casual setting. We'll probably have to talk, and people might figure out that we used to know each other. I don't want to have to answer a bunch of questions.

Oh, I should stop writing. I'm over at Mary's and one of her boys is screaming out in the yard.

12:30 p.m.

Vivian

Dear Diary,

Willoughby is amazing. We've been officially dating for two whole days now and he is so adorable!!

Actually, I'm not sure that anything is really "official" between us. But we met three days ago and the next day was when I twisted my ankle and he carried me home. Then he kissed me later that afternoon when he came over to check on me, so that's what I'm going to use as the beginning of our relationship. We don't really need to talk about stuff like if we're a couple or not. We both just know. It was definitely love at first sight and it's even more wonderful than I ever imagined it would be.

I've never liked a guy so much before. Not even close to this. He's a total romantic! Yesterday he brought me wildflowers from a meadow near his house. It was seriously the sweetest thing ever.

Tomorrow we're going out to dinner and then we're driving into the city to see the new Wes Anderson movie. I love that we both love the same kinds of offbeat stuff. He introduced me to this Scottish band called Frightened Rabbit, and now I absolutely worship them. And we both love Miyazaki movies. And poetry! Last night he read me some of his favorite poems and they were so good! He has such a nice reading voice, so much expression and vivacity. He really knows how to make things come alive when he's reading. I could listen to him read poetry all day long.

Love from a totally smitten,

Vivian

3:00 p.m.

♥ *N*ila ♥

*D*ear *T*aylor,

My plan is working! I invited Priyam, Elton, Amar, and a few other people to come over and rewatch *The Fault in Our Stars* at my house last night, so Priyam and Elton finally got to meet! I think they really like each other! After Priyam left, I texted her to see if she'd had a good time and ask her what she thought about Elton. She seems really into him. And why wouldn't she be? He was so friendly to her the whole night, and they sat next to each other on the couch—I arranged that, by the way. I am so good at this matchmaking thing.

At first Elton sat down next to me, but then I said I needed to go check on my dad, who was upstairs the whole time. And when I got back, I sat down next to Amar and told Priyam she should take my spot on the couch instead of lying on the floor because her back has been hurting.

It took her a second to catch on, but finally it worked and then Priyam and Elton spent the whole night practically snuggled up together on the couch.

I am brilliant.

Anyway, I'll keep you updated on this budding romance. Hope you're having fun!

Love ya,

Nila

4:00 p.m.

Anne

So, I guess I'm not going to dinner at the Musgroves after all. I just spent the entire afternoon in the emergency room waiting area with my nephew Walter. He fell out of a tree and hit his head. He's okay now, but someone needs to stay home and watch him, and I think it's going to be me.

Charles already promised to help his family with the dinner and Mary really wants to go, so I said I'd stay. Charles and Mary are still arguing about it in the other room, but I know what the outcome will be.

On the one hand, I feel relieved that I don't have to see Mr. Wentworth. But I am sort of curious about what he's like now. It's been so long since I had a real conversation with him. I wonder if he's still the same person I remember.

Anyway, I should go check on Walter. Poor little guy. He was a trooper through the whole ordeal. He had to get stitches and everything.

—A.E.

9:00 p.m.

FIONA

I have really bad news. My dad got a new job. Okay, that probably sounds like good news. And it is, technically. According to my stepmom, "it's a great career move for him," which basically means he'll be making more money. That's good. I'm glad he won't have to stress so much about our finances anymore.

But the job he got is in Antigua. I didn't even know where that was until I looked it up online. Turns out it's an island in the Caribbean, which sounds really nice—for *him*.

Because apparently he's moving there without me. And without his wife. And his stepkids. And I'm supposed to just stay here with all of them. My stepmom isn't too happy about it either. She even mentioned sending me back to live with my mom.

Let me make it clear, I would LOVE to go live with my mom. But my dad won't even talk about it as an option. I don't know all the details, but I do know that when I was ten, he went through a crazy custody battle to get me and my brother away from my mom. Now he won't even let me visit her.

And I haven't seen my brother, William, in ages. He's in college on the other side of the country and he doesn't even come home for the holidays.

I feel like my family is falling apart. I can't lose my dad too. I hate my life.

EIGHT

MONDAY, 9/5

Labor Day

9:00 a.m.

Anne

So the good news is that Walter is doing much better. He dislocated his collarbone, but all he wants to do is go run around outside. Typical boy. We're trying our best to keep him occupied indoors. So far the only thing that seems to be working is his Wii. But even that involves a little too much movement sometimes. Poor kid.

And the bad news? Well, according to Mary, both Louisa and Henrietta Musgrove were flirting with Mr. Wentworth all night at dinner. Mary and Charles have a bet going now about who Mr. Wentworth is more interested in.

Mary doesn't know, by the way, about my history with Fred. She was too young to pick up on what was going on in my life when I was in high school, and Elizabeth has never filled her in on the details. They don't talk much. And when they do it's about what's trending on YouTube and which all-natural herbal remedies will heal Mary's various symptoms.

But somehow I guess the fact that Mr. Wentworth used to know me came up at dinner. According to Mary, they all asked him what he thought of me now and he said, "She's so different. I almost didn't recognize her."

Yeah. That's the really bad news.

Am I different? And why should I care what he thinks? It's not like I'm expecting anything to happen now. That was all over years ago.

But still. It bugs me.

Why would he say that? I swear I don't look very different. I mean, yes, I'm getting older. I may have put on a couple pounds since high school, when I was super thin. But no one stays the same forever.

Except, he did. He looks just like he did in high school, only more handsome. Instead of looking like a cute boy, he looks like a mature distinguished man. With just a hint of scruff. Ugh.

I know, I know. I should just stop. None of this is helping.

—A.E.

10:00 a.m.

Lizzie

Three-day weekends are the best!

Today is Labor Day, which means we don't have school and I don't have to see Caroline or Liam or any of the other people that make Pemberley such a "charming" place to be educated. Not that Liam goes to Pemberley. Obviously.

The point is—I'm free!! Today I'm hanging out with Charlotte all day. She's coming over for lunch and then we're going to redecorate my room. Now that Jane has officially moved out of the house, I can finally get rid of the unicorn wallpaper we've had up since I was six. Jane still loves that unicorn wallpaper.

But she's at Mansfield this weekend, spending time with Charles Bingley, so now is my chance to strike. And, honestly, once she gets over the initial shock, I'm sure Jane won't mind. I'll save her a section of wallpaper as a memento.

I am so glad I have my own room! I love Jane, of course. But I have waited years for this day. I already picked out several options for a new paint color. I just can't decide if I want something more neutral, like gray, or something fun, like coral or turquoise.

And then for dinner my whole family is going over to the Lucases for a big BBQ, and Charlotte said I could text Wickham and invite him to come, so with any luck, I'll get to spend the entire evening flirting with him!

Yes!

That is, I'll get to flirt with him for as long as I can keep him away from Lydia. So . . . maybe for about fifteen minutes total all night.

Ha! Look at that. I wrote an entire journal entry without ranting once.

Better quit while I'm ahead.

TUESDAY, 9/6

7:00 p.m.

Vivian

Dear Diary,

Today I told Alice about my first kiss with Willoughby. It wasn't exactly my first kiss ever. There was that boy Marco in fifth grade that I kissed once because my friend Phoebe dared me to. And then in seventh grade I went to this summer writing camp in San Francisco. And I met this guy there—Ian—that I sort of dated for like a week while we were both at the camp. I mean, we never actually went out on a date or anything. But we would sit together and read each other our poetry. He was pretty nice. At the end of the week, he kissed me good-bye. But then I found out that he got back together with his girlfriend three days later.

Anyway. I don't know why I'm talking about Marco and Ian when I could be telling you more about Willoughby. We've been texting back and forth all day today, and he is hilarious and super sweet. He keeps asking if my ankle feels better yet. And I keep telling him that it's fine now.

But I will never forget how it felt when he carried me to safety. He is the most amazing guy I've ever known. I can't believe he likes me back!!! I know we're young, but we're perfect together. I want to spend forever with him.

Love,

Vivian Willoughby

Aw! I love the way that sounds! I could totally become a famous poet with a name like that!

8:00 p.m.

Alice-

This is bad. This is really, really bad. Vivian has fallen for a guy again—completely fallen for him. She's in way over her head.

I thought she'd outgrown her boy-crazy phase. She definitely hasn't seemed so swoony since our dad died. I had hoped she was becoming more mature and that she had finally come to her senses about boys. But apparently she's just as hopeless as ever. This thing with Willoughby is moving way too fast. I don't even know his first name, but according to Vivian he is "perfect" and they're "in love."

How can you fall in love with someone after three days? I just wish she'd be a little more careful. She's so emotional that if something feels right to her, she'll just go for it. No thinking. Just leaping.

I could never do that. How does she know this guy won't turn out to be a horrible person? How does she even know that she likes him? I've known Peter for years and sometimes I still have no idea how I really feel about him. Not that I like Peter. I don't. Of course I don't like Peter. I can't like him because . . . Well, I just can't.

Never mind Peter. I can't talk about him right now. I have to figure out how to stop Vivian before something terrible happens.

She's just so young. She's only a freshman. I wanted her first year at Pemberley to be full of fun things like volunteering with Habitat for Humanity and group video projects for Mrs. Jennings's history class. I didn't want her to get caught up in all of this boy stuff until she was at least sixteen. Maybe not even then.

I wish my dad were still alive. I'm sure he would know what to do. My mom just keeps gushing about how cute Willoughby is and how sweet it is that he came to Viv's rescue. Honestly, my mom is as bad as Vivian.

I don't know what to do!

NINE

WEDNESDAY, 9/7

1:30 p.m.

FIONA

I'm not at school today. I wasn't feeling well this morning, so my dad said I could stay home and help him get ready for his move. I'm still really mad at him for leaving, but I want to enjoy all the time I have with him before he goes.

I keep getting this horrible feeling like I'm never going to see him again. I wonder what would happen if he died. Would my stepmom even let me stay here? Maybe I would *have* to go live with my mom. I might not have any other choice. Or maybe I could move in with my brother William somehow. I think he lives in a dorm right now, but we could get an apartment together. It wouldn't have to be luxurious or anything as long as we could be together. I know he'd take care of me and that he'd love me. I don't know if anyone except my dad and William actually love me.

My stepmom and stepsiblings all *need* me—they need me to make them dinner and help them find things around the house and make sure all the laundry gets done.

And in some ways it's nice to be needed. It's almost like being loved, but it's not really the same thing.

Anyway, it's been cool to spend time with my dad and have the house to ourselves for once. We've been sorting through piles of his stuff all morning. He's already packed a lot of boxes that he's planning to ship to Antigua. Earlier, I was helping him look at apartments there. He wanted to get one with two bedrooms so he'd have room for us to stay if we come and visit him, but I reminded him that we don't have any money to travel.

That's the whole reason he's moving there—to earn enough money for all six of us to go to college: Tom, William, Edmund, Mariah, me, and Julia. Yet another problem with blended families: you can end up with a lot of kids who are all close to the same age and all need to go to college at the same time. Luckily William already has a scholarship and Edmund and I will probably be able to get some scholarship money too, but the others won't.

Unless they give out scholarships for partying. Mariah could definitely get one of those.

3:00 p.m.

♥ Nila ♥

Dear Taylor,

This is so exciting! I just got a text from Elton. He wants me to set up a photo shoot for Priyam! Isn't that adorable? He must really like her. I mentioned to both of them the other day that I used to do photo shoots with you, and Elton said he'd love to

help with one. Priyam is going to be such a cute model! I'm so excited!

I think we'll go out to that old barn on Hartfield Road. With the fall scenery and Priyam in my riding boots, these photos are going to look stunning.

In other news, Amar is being weird and cryptic lately. Well, weirder and more cryptic than usual. I think he thinks I'm going overboard with this whole Priyam thing. But he just hasn't spent enough time with her. She really is darling.

Of course, no one will ever replace you in my heart. But I know you'd want me to have friends. Just like I hope you've made some good friends there to keep you company while we're separated.

Your bff (obvs),

Nila

3:30 p.m.

Lizzie

I will not—I repeat—I Will. Not. Go to the Darcys' beach house this weekend. I don't care if Jane thinks she's coming down with something. If she were really sick, she would stay here and try to recover.

Instead she said to me, "But, Lizzie, I need you to be there with me! What if my cold gets worse and there's no one to make me lemon and honey tea? What if I lose my voice or something? You know you're the only one who can read my hand signals!"

This is actually true. When we were little, Jane and

I came up with our own version of sign language to use around our family so our little sisters wouldn't know what we were talking about. It worked really well until one day when Lydia decided to start screaming any time we signaled to each other. Lydia gets feisty when she feels excluded.

Anyway, as much as I love Jane, I hate the Darcys even more. That is why this weekend I will be happily whiling away my time here in good old Kensington while Jane is off taking long walks on the beach with Charles.

I really hope he doesn't break her heart. I still don't trust that guy. How can Liam Darcy's best friend be anything but evil?

4:00 p.m.

Cate

You won't believe what I just found out.

Henry's sister is in my PE class! Can you believe that? All this time I've practically been stalking him at that boutique store and I could've just been talking to his sister in PE. This is why you should always find out what your crush's last name is as soon as possible.

Well, now I know. Henry's last name is Tilney. And Eleanor Tilney is my new gym class running buddy.

Here's what happened: Yesterday I happened to see Henry in the school parking lot, picking up a girl I recognized from PE. So today when we were running laps I asked her if she had a boyfriend. And she said she didn't.

(Phew.) So I asked her who that guy was that picked her up. And she said it was her brother, Henry.

Crazy, right?

Here's some more stuff I found out about Henry:

He's a junior at Donwell High. He works at the boutique on the weekends, but most of the time he just works in the back, stocking things. That must be why I didn't see him when I went there all those times, looking for him. They just moved back to this area, so Eleanor is new at Pemberley this year just like I am, except she went to elementary school here so she knows some people from back then.

I really like Eleanor. I hope we become better friends. And I don't just hope that because she's Henry's sister. Although, I'm not going to lie—that definitely has something to do with it. But I'd like Eleanor anyway. She's really nice and down-to-earth, you know? I feel like I can talk to her about serious things. That can be hard to find in a friend.

Anyway, I need to go tell Bella everything I found out. She's been bugging me to update her on the Henry situation and this is a major breakthrough.

TEN

FRIDAY, 9/9

3:00 p.m.

ALICE-

I just got into a huge almost-fight with Vivian.

She accused me of being jealous. I am not.

She also thinks I'm being paranoid. I don't think so.

I just explained to her that it would be wise to get to know someone a little better before you let him drag you off to Napa for an entire weekend, where cell reception might not be great and no one could hear you scream from the middle of a vineyard.

Does that sound like paranoia to you? I like to think of it as caution. And for good reason. After all, none of us really know this Willoughby guy. He only showed up in our lives a week ago. And just because he and Vivian have been inseparable since then is no reason for us to trust him.

All right. Fine. I don't really think he's a murderer.

I will admit that he actually seems pretty cool. Vivian obviously loves him. My mom is charmed. Even Amy has fallen under his spell. I have to admit, he has very good manners. And he definitely knows how to say the right thing. But he's almost too good-looking, you know?

I just don't want to see Vivian get hurt—physically, emotionally, whatever. I want her to remain completely unhurt in all ways.

And in my experience, any time people fall in love, it ends with someone getting hurt.

5:00 p.m.

Lizzie

Guess where I am right now.

Did you say sitting in the backseat of Charles Bingley's vintage Corvette on my way to the Darcys' beach house in picturesque Carmel-by-the-Sea? Then you're right. Oh, wait . . . you didn't say that? Weird.

Yeah, that is soooo not what I would've said either.

I can't believe this is happening. I don't want to believe it. The whole thing feels like a nightmare. Maybe if I'm lucky, we'll get hit by a rogue tsunami or something and all my troubles will be over.

Okay, okay. I'm not actually suicidal. As much as Liam Darcy bugs me, I wouldn't kill myself just to avoid spending time with him. But mostly because I wouldn't want to give him the satisfaction of knowing that he bothers me that much.

Anyway, the good news is that Charles is actually a nice guy. Surprising, I know, considering who his sister and friend are, but it's true. I really like him. He's funny and nice and so sweet to Jane. I approve.

Charles is the one bright spot in this completely insane weekend. Why do I let myself get sucked into these things? Why?

Do you think there's some way I can avoid everyone except for Jane and Charles the whole time? I'm going to do my best.

Later

8:30 p.m.

Just when I thought things couldn't get any worse, the power went out. I am not kidding. I'm literally writing by candlelight right now.

This house is massive, by the way. I should've known it would be. But with the storm going on outside and no heater in here, it's not much fun being at the beach. At least we've got a fire going so we won't freeze to death.

Right now we're all hanging out in the family room around the only heat source, and with nothing better to do, we've resorted to playing cards. Well, some people are playing cards: Caroline; her sister, May; and May's boyfriend. I played with them for a little bit, but I'm not really into that sort of thing.

May and her boyfriend, Hurst, are supposed to be chaperoning all of us. But it's pretty obvious that they're only here for the free food and drinks. We don't really need chaperoning. Caroline and I are the youngest ones here, and except for us and Liam, everyone else is in college. I think the Darcys just wanted to make sure we had someone over age twenty-three with us. Apparently May's boyfriend qualifies.

But aside from his age, he seems totally useless. He actually screamed when the lights went out. May is a lot like Caroline, but older and not quite as pretty. She seems just as competitive though. Even when the only thing to compete in is a pointless card game.

Jane and Charles are curled up on a couch together, being their super-cute-couple selves.

And Liam is reading.

Oh, this is weird. Caroline just asked me to walk around the room with her. Why?

Later

So . . . this just happened:

Caroline: Liam, why don't you come walk with us?

Liam: No thanks.

Caroline: Are you sure? Aren't you sick of just sitting around? I wish it weren't raining. What's the point of coming to the beach if all we do is sit around inside? This trip sucks!

Me: We could just go home early.

At this point everyone looked at me like I was crazy. Except Jane who gave me a pleading look.

Caroline: Why would we do that?

Me: Never mind.

Caroline: Come on, Liam. Just walk around with us. Or we could play a different game or something.

Liam: I'm busy. Besides, I'd just be in your way.

Caroline: What do you mean? Lizzie, do you know what he's talking about?

Liam: Well, obviously you're either walking around so you can whisper your girl secrets to each other or you're doing it so you can show off how you look. If it's to gossip, I'd be in your way. And if not, I can see your figures much better from my comfortable chair here by the fire.

Let me just interrupt this recap for a second to say, "figures?" What the crap? Who talks like that?

Caroline: Liam! You're terrible! Lizzie, how should we get back at him?

Me: Oh, uh, I'm sure you must know what to tease him about. You know him a lot better than I do.

Caroline: But what is there to tease him about? He's so calm and thoughtful all the time.

Me: Seriously? Liam Darcy has no faults? That's too bad. I'm glad my friends aren't perfect. It'd make life very boring.

Liam: Caroline's exaggerating. Of course I have faults, but I try to avoid the weaknesses I see in other people.

Me: Like pride?

Liam: I don't think pride is a weakness. Not when you actually have a superior mind.

Me: Oh. Wow. Okay then.

Caroline: Are you satisfied now? I told you there was nothing to tease him about.

Me: Yep. You're right. He has no faults. He pretty much said so himself.

Liam: I did *not* say that. And I do have faults. I get angry sometimes. Actually, resentful is a better word. It takes me a long time to get over things.

Me: Huh. Well, it's kind of hard to laugh about that.

Liam: Actually, I think everybody has one specific fault that they're especially prone to. I'm always looking for it in the people I meet.

Me: Really? I guess that means your one fault is a tendency to look for the worst in people.

Liam: And your one fault is to twist people's intentions around on purpose.

Caroline: Okay, you two, that's enough arguing. Liam! I just remembered you have a piano here. Can I play it? May, you don't mind if I wake up Hurst, do you? I think he fell asleep on the couch over there.

So now Caroline's playing the piano loudly, Darcy and I have retreated to our separate corners, and things have sort of gone back to normal.

But seriously. I hate Liam Darcy. He's such an arrogant jerk. And he's glad to be that way. That's the worst part. Not only is he stuck up, but he's not sorry about it. He's actually proud of how proud he is. Ugh.

I can't believe I'm stuck with him for two more days. I will be so glad when this weekend is over.

Maybe I'll call home in the morning and see if my dad will come pick me up. Assuming my phone doesn't die before then.

ELEVEN

SATURDAY, 9/10

1:30 p.m.

Cate

Something's bothering Bella. I tried to tell her all about meeting Eleanor Tilney and it was like she wasn't even listening. We were sitting in her room, and I'm pretty sure her younger sisters were listening right outside the door, but whatever. And Bella was doing her nails, except she kept having to stop because she'd get a text from someone and obviously it's pretty difficult to paint your nails and text at the same time. Anyway, we kept getting interrupted by one thing or another and then when I finally finished my story, Bella went, "So?"

Hmpf. Not exactly the reaction I was hoping for. But I guess I can see why it wouldn't be as big of a deal to her as it is to me. After all, she's not the one who has a crush on Henry. In fact, she's never even met him. Maybe I should invite Bella and Eleanor over to watch a movie with me sometime, so at least the two of them could meet. And maybe Eleanor would just happen to bring Henry with her. Hey, a girl can dream, right? Or I could be really bold and tell Eleanor that I like her brother.

Uh . . . nope. Not gonna happen. That sounds like something a girl in a book would do. And I am no heroine.

4:00 p.m.

Vivian

Dear Diary,

Alice is driving me crazy.

She's been bugging me to join her list of tutors for her after-school project. Now that I'm in high school, I'm old enough to do it. And, of course, I really do want to help her. She does a lot for me and my mom and Amy, but . . . sometimes she does too much, you know? Like, I just want to tell her, "You don't have to take care of us all. We can handle things on our own. Maybe we won't handle them exactly the way you would and, yeah, we might get a little more emotional than you do about stuff, but we can still handle it, in our own way."

I don't know. I just don't want Alice to put her whole life on hold because she feels like she has to take care of everyone else before herself.

And this community tutoring thing is a good idea, but it keeps her really busy. I can't remember the last time Alice went to a party or just hung out with her friends. I'm not even sure she has any friends anymore. She's too busy volunteering at homeless shelters on the weekends, and she spends her Friday nights doing extra credit. Oh, actually, she does have Lucy. Alice says they're friends, but I think Lucy's more like a leech. Maybe they really are friends, though, and that's who Alice confides in. She certainly doesn't confide in me.

I'm not jealous, I just hope she has someone to talk to about how she's feeling because I don't think it's healthy to keep everything bottled up inside.

Plus, this whole thing with Peter makes me nuts. Neither one of them is brave enough to face their feelings but I think they could be really happy together. Just like me and Willoughby.

Things are still going great with him, by the way. We're planning to go visit his aunt in Napa next weekend. Alice almost forbid me from going, but luckily my mom intervened. Alice is worried about the two of us going on an overnight trip together when we "barely know each other," but it's not like anything's going to happen.

Willoughby's aunt just has a really cool house and he wants to show it to me. And we're staying in separate guest rooms, so seriously, it's no big deal. But Alice gave me this endlessly long lecture a couple of days ago about propriety and not exposing myself to the gossip of others. We almost got into a fight about it. Sometimes I think Alice was born in the wrong century.

Besides, I don't care what other people say or what they think. Willoughby and I both know we were meant to be, and even if the whole world came down on us, we'd still have each other. That's all I need to know.

Love from a smiling,

Vivian

5:00 p.m.

FIONA

Well, my dad is gone. He left for his new job, and I'm trying to be happy for him. But it's so weird not having him around the house.

I didn't really think of my dad as being a very influential person in our family. Like, yes, he's sort of in charge and stuff, but it's not like he was home all that much before. He was always busy working. And besides, he's a lot quieter than my stepmom, so it's easier to notice her influence, I guess.

But now that he's gone, I can see how much my dad really did for all of us. He always helped me with the dishes after dinner, and he made sure that the house was locked up at night. He was the first one up in the morning, so he turned on the coffee maker and yelled up the stairs if it took us too long to get out of bed. I don't know. It's not like any of those things are hard to do, but I miss having him here to do them.

Julia and Mariah have already started to get worse. Their rooms are even messier somehow. I didn't think that was possible.

And Tom decided to stay at our house this weekend, instead of at Mansfield. It's not like that's a bad thing, except that Tom's loud and rude, and he plays video games. Like a lot. Really violent ones with booming explosions that echo through our whole house. And now that my dad's not here, Tom thinks it's fine to just hang around all the time and yell at his mom and me.

The only person who could ever really keep Tom in line was my dad. Edmund tries, but how much can a younger brother do?

Still, I hate to think what it would be like around here if we didn't have Edmund looking out for us.

6:30 p.m.

Lizzie

My dad did not come pick me up. But he did pass the message on to my mom, who then went completely crazy! She decided that the best thing to do in this situation would be to come check on me and Jane. With all three of my younger sisters in tow. Not even joking.

They drove the two and a half hours out here to the Darcys' house just to make sure I was okay. Because obviously a simple phone call would not have been sufficient.

So this afternoon I had to endure the most awkward conversation ever while my mom tried to make small talk with Charles and Liam. And the whole time Caroline and May were off in one corner just laughing to themselves—allegedly about something they were reading in a magazine—but I can tell you that was so not the case.

They were laughing at us, at me and my family. They think they're so much better than us, just because they have money and live in a gated community. It's ridiculous.

Then Jane, who had been in the shower this whole time (lucky her), came downstairs and said, "Oh, hi, Mom." Like it was no big deal that she was here. As much as I love her, Jane is sometimes so clueless about social norms. I think it's because in her mind everyone is just as nice and transparent as she is.

The absolute worst part came at the end. I was all ready to just leave with my mom, but then Jane was like, "Well, I should probably come with you too."

And so my mom—who would do anything to keep Jane around Charles a little longer—was like, "Oh, no, we can't take you girls home. We don't have room in our car. We just came to make sure you were all right."

What!?!

So now I'm stuck here for at least another twenty-four hours. And everyone else is having such a good time that they're talking about skipping school on Monday to stay an extra day at the beach.

So I told them, "No way. I can't stay. I have a test coming up and I really need to be back at school."

Caroline looked at me like I was such a nerd. Then Liam piped up and said, "Well, if you really need to be there, I could drive you back and we could let the others stay. I shouldn't miss school either."

Yeah right. I'd miss an entire semester of school if the alternative was spending multiple hours alone in a car with Liam.

I wish Wickham were here. I texted him earlier to tell him where I was and he just texted back:

> "That sucks! Don't let the Darcys get you down. And come back soon! I miss you!"

He's so cute.

9:00 p.m.

♥ *Nila* ♥

Dear Taylor,

The photo shoot went really well!

Actually, the photos aren't all that great. The lighting wasn't cooperating, and I realized I'm really out of practice when it comes to little things like framing my shots and picking the best lens. I mean, they came out okay, but I've done better. I wish you'd been here. You were the one who taught me all this photography stuff in the first place.

But, anyway, the real success of the day was how much Elton and Priyam flirted. They're so cute! Priyam's still really shy around him, so I had to keep encouraging her to talk more, but Elton obviously likes her. He was so helpful the whole day. He kept asking me if there was anything else he could do for her.

Then when we were done, we went back to my house to have pizza, and Elton insisted that I show Priyam all the photos we'd taken. So we went through every single shot and for each one, Elton had something nice to say.

Priyam was practically glowing from all the praise. I really think she likes him. I just wish there was more I could do. We're all going to a movie together next weekend. It's supposed to be the three of us, but maybe I could cancel at the last minute, and then the two of them could just go together. Like a date. It'd be perfect!

Okay. Good plan. I will let you know how it goes.

Love,

Nila

TWELVE

SUNDAY, 9/11

9:00 p.m.

Lizzie

Finally! This crazy, stupid weekend is over.

Okay, okay. It wasn't actually that bad. Still, I am sooooo happy to be back in my own bed! I never realized how comforting the sound of Lydia and Kitty giggling together was. Of course, they can be giggling one minute and screaming at each other the next, but I'll take it any day over the sound of the ocean waves crashing into the rocks at the Darcys'. Because it was So. Quiet. There that I'm pretty sure I heard every single wave in all seventy-two of those hours.

Liam Darcy just has that effect on people. They're so disturbed by his solemnity that they forget to keep breathing, let alone speaking.

Anyway, I'm tired of talking about Darcy.

Let's talk about how I hardly got any homework done this weekend and I have a huge history test on Friday and I'm probably going to spend this entire week studying! Blech!

Okay, let's not talk about that either. Too stressful.

In fact, instead of talking about studying, I should probably just go actually study. I'll feel better about my life if I can check off something on my to-do list.

Yep. That's what I'm gonna do. Okay . . . now to find the motivation to stop writing and actually get off the couch.

And one, two, three . . . go.

Didn't work.

Still here.

And . . .

Ugh! Okay! One last thing. I wasn't even going to write this down but whatever.

As I was packing my things into Charles's car for the drive home, Liam came up behind me and helped me lift one of my suitcases into the car and for a second there we were really, really close to each other and then I turned to look up at him and he was giving me this look.

I've never seen him make that face before. He looked . . . like he was about to smile but he had forgotten how to do it. And it was . . . I don't know. It was weird. But it was a different kind of weird. And then we both just sort of looked away. And things went back to normal.

So . . . I don't know what's up with that. I don't even know why I wrote it down. I guess I'm just stalling as long as I possibly can to avoid all the studying I need to do.

But, seriously, I should go now.

MONDAY, 9/12

10:00 a.m.

♥ Nila ♥

Dear Taylor,

It's Monday morning and it's foggy and dull outside. I'm in history and Mrs. Jennings is droning on and on and on. I'm supposed to be taking notes, but I decided to write to you instead. That's much more fun.

I wish you were here to cheer me up. It's such a blah day outside and it's making me feel emotionally blah too. Normally I don't mind the fog, but sometimes it just gets to you. Actually, you probably get a lot of fog in London too, right? I think the Thames is famous for it. Or something like that. Except I'm pretty sure my main idea of what London is like is coming from the descriptions we had to find in Oliver Twist. Do you remember when we had that assignment last year? Neither of us knew then that you'd actually be living in London!

By the way, I loved all the photos you posted of your weekend trip to Paris. You are SO lucky! I can't imagine wandering around cobblestone streets and alleyways and munching on croissants at a café. It sounds like a dream. Or like a super chic Audrey Hepburn movie. Without all the gross smoking.

Nothing much is happening here. I'm almost finished editing all of the photos of Priyam that I took on Saturday. Elton texted me last night from San Francisco. He went all the way there to get a frame for his favorite photo from the shoot. See? This just proves that he loves Priyam.

I can't believe Amar still doesn't see it. He's insane.

Anyway, I have to go. We only have fifteen minutes left in history and I need to finish doing my math homework before next period.

Why does school have to involve so much homework? Oh well.

Talk to you more soon!

Love always,

Nila

Lunch

Anne

I've been avoiding this journal for a while now. I'd still rather not talk about what's going on, but I think maybe I should just face the facts. If I actually see them written down, it might make it easier to deal with them. Might.

So, here's the deal. I'm fairly certain that Louisa Musgrove would like to be dating Mr. Wentworth. And Louisa is a very determined person. If anyone could make this happen, she could. Today Louisa and I carpooled together and as we were leaving school, we happened to see Mr. Wentworth in the parking lot. Louisa immediately started gushing about him, and then she walked over to him and they stood there chatting for a solid ten minutes, at which point, I finally got tired of waiting for her and went and sat in the car. The entire way home, he was all she could talk about.

Apparently he's been to their house twice in the past

week. I guess Mary and Charles were right to place bets on which of the Musgroves Fred is interested in. Reading between the lines of Louisa's stories about him, it seems like Fred—I mean, Mr. Wentworth—is definitely interested in either her or Henrietta. Or at least he pays them both enough attention that the rest of the family notices and talks about it.

So, where does that leave me? Should I stop going over to the Musgroves in case I see him there? Or should I keep going over so that I can get used to being around him?

After all, with a little more practice, I hope I'd start to be less awkward in his presence. And if he's going to be dating one of the Musgroves, I should try to be less awkward because I probably will be seeing him. Not to mention the fact that I'll still have to see him around school.

Yeah. I should just suck it up and learn how to face him. It's been eight years, after all. I shouldn't have to change my life just because he happened to show up again.

Okay.

Okay. Now I know what I have to do. And that's good because Louisa just called to invite me to a barbecue at her family's house tomorrow night. And I can guarantee that Mr. Wentworth will be there.

I said I'd go. I just wish I wasn't so nervous about it.

—A.E.

TUESDAY, 9/13

6:00 p.m.

Cate

The strangest thing about living in Kensington is how few people I know. It's not like this is a very big town. It's almost more like a neighborhood. But unlike home in Idaho, no one seems to know their neighbors here. I mean, you might know their names, but you don't get together and talk to them, except maybe one or two families.

For the Allens, it's the Thorpes. They're the only neighbors we have that we would just drop in on unannounced.

At home, we know the Coopers, the Smiths, the Grangers, the Nelsons, the Bartholomews, the Winegars, and the Ellistons, and that's only the people who live on our street. Also, we have a lot more space around our houses. When I first moved here I thought all the houses here were so close together because they're old. But the other day when we went to Mansfield, we drove past a brand-new development of houses and they were building them even closer together than they are here. So apparently the problem is getting worse, not better.

How can people live like that, with no yard space? I can't imagine not having any grass to lie down in or plants to grow. It would be such a sad, seasonless life. How would you know when spring was coming if you didn't have crocuses and daffodils to tell you?

That's another thing. I don't think there's going to be

a winter here. All of the plants are still in bloom, and the weather is still just as warm as it was when I moved here. According to Mr. Allen, there are only two seasons here instead of four: a dry season and a wet season. He says the wet season doesn't even start till December or January. This is such a strange place.

I guess it will be nice not having to wear snow boots and big winter coats. But I'll miss sledding and all the fall colors and icicles and going skating on the Martins' pond.

At least I'm going home for Christmas break. I'll just have to get my fill of winter in those two weeks.

THIRTEEN

WEDNESDAY, 9/14

3:30 p.m.

FIONA

Something really strange is going on. Two days ago I came home from school to find a note for me tucked into our front door. It said "Will." That's it. Then yesterday I found a note addressed to me in my locker and all it said was "you." And now I just got home from school and there's a note on my bed that says, "go."

I know this is going to sound crazy, but if you put them together it's, "Will you go . . ." and that could end up being something like, "Will you go out with me?"

But I have no idea who would send me a message like that. And they have to be for me—they have my name on them and everything. And who could've gotten into our house to put a note like that on my bed? Unless . . .

No. I won't even let myself think it.

But . . .

No. It's not possible.

It's just that . . .

No. There is no way he would do that.

Okay. To avoid arguing with myself any more, I'm

going to write this down, just once, and then I swear to myself I will never even entertain the thought of it ever again.

But what if they're from Edmund?

He wouldn't have had to sneak into our house because he lives here. And, yes, I know we're stepsiblings and it would probably cause both my dad and my stepmom to have separate and collective heart attacks if we were to start dating, but let me just explain something: I've never thought of Edmund as a brother. He's always been more like a best friend that just happens to live in the same house as I do. William is my real brother, and I'm close with him too, even though he never comes home. But we skype and text all the time. I know how I feel about William, and that's not at all the same as how I feel about Edmund.

Edmund is kind to me. He takes care of me. He's always looking out for me. I think I've kind of been in love with him since the moment I met him.

I can't believe I'm even writing this down. Everyone would freak out if they knew.

I just needed to get it out of my system.

And now that I've started thinking about it, I can't stop. These notes are making it worse. What if Edmund really is trying to tell me something? What if he feels the same way I do?

What if—? Okay. What am I talking about? I know he doesn't feel the same. He likes Mary. He has flat-out told me he likes Mary.

But I can't figure out who else would be sending me

notes like this. At first I thought it was some kind of practical joke. Maybe it is. I don't know.

I'm freaking out.

Normally if something like this were happening, I'd go talk to Edmund about it. But I obviously can't do that right now. Maybe I'll try asking Julia and Mariah if they know anything about it. After all, someone in our house has to be in on it. How else would this last note have made it onto my bed?

This is just so weird.

And scary. And wrong. Whatever. I'm just going to ignore all this and hope it goes away.

Maybe if I don't respond to these notes, whoever is sending them will decide to just leave me alone.

4:30 p.m.

ALICE-

I hate to say this in case I jinx it, but I just got out of a meeting and I think we finalized all the preparations for our back-to-school dance.

The dance is next Friday, so I'll be extra busy for the next ten days, but it'll be worth it. I think it's going to be the best dance Pemberley or Donwell has ever had.

Peter came to the meeting. Normally Amar is there as the Donwell student body rep, but Amar had a doctor's appointment today, so Peter came instead. It was nice to see him. We didn't get to talk much because I was so busy with official business, but he looked good.

Sometimes I worry about Peter. His mom puts a lot of

pressure on him, and I know he wants to make her happy, but his priorities are different than hers.

He gets good grades and he works really hard, but that's not what's important to her. She'd rather have him get mediocre grades if it meant he was more popular. I know she wants him to join the basketball team. Peter's never been into sports, but his family can't see that. They're still expecting him to become a star athlete any day now. Even Lucy seems to be expecting that.

I don't want to talk about Lucy.

I wish I could show them all what I see in him. Peter is smart and responsible. He goes out of his way to take care of the people around him. He's been a tutor in my program for years, and he helps with lots of other volunteer projects too. And he does it because he genuinely cares, not because he's trying to make himself look better on his college applications.

He's probably the most selfless person I know. He's just not the kind of person who would ever want to be in the spotlight.

That's why most people don't notice him.

But I do.

THURSDAY, 9/15

7:00 p.m.

Lizzie

Ms. Elliot, if you're reading this, I'm sorry I haven't written in here much this week. I've been super busy cramming for Mrs. Jennings's big history test. I have to do well on it. And if I can't do well, I at least have to do better than Caroline.

Also, there's not much to tell you about my life right now. Wickham is still hilarious via text, but I haven't seen him much in real life. We've both been too busy with school stuff.

Jane and Charles are still a thing. I thought for sure that my mom showing up in the middle of our beach weekend would scare Charles off, but I guess when he and Jane are at Mansfield, he can somehow forget about her crazy family long enough to keep asking her out.

I'm happy for them. I've decided Charles is kind of perfect for her. He's sweet and kind. He's always bringing her flowers or little presents. Yesterday she texted me to say that he left a giant teddy bear outside her dorm room. Personally, that's a little too much for me. But Jane loves that sort of thing.

If only Charles wasn't related to Caroline. Then I really would like him.

Oh well. I guess we can't choose who we're related to. If we could, I would not have any younger sisters. Just saying.

Okay. Back to the Napoleonic wars. I will be SO glad when this test is over.

Who even cares what happened in 1813? That was, like, two hundred years ago.

8:00 p.m.

Vivian

Dear Diary,

I can't believe that in just forty-eight hours, I will be in Napa spending a romantic weekend with the love of my life! Could things possibly get any better?

I think not!!

Sigh. I am so ready for this mini-vacation. I just want to get away from everything: my math homework, all the planning that's going into the back-to-school dance, and especially Alice's nagging voice in the back of my head.

All I want to do is lie out in the sun next to the pool at Willoughby's aunt's house and maybe go horseback riding. Apparently there are stables nearby. Doesn't that sound so cool? The only time I've ever been horseback riding was with my dad when I was ten. And all we did was walk in a big circle around a field.

I wonder what my dad would think of Willoughby.

Hm . . . I think he would approve.

Actually, in some ways Willoughby sort of reminds me of my dad.

My dad was a take-charge sort of person. He was confident but also very caring.

That's how Willoughby is too. When I fell and twisted my ankle, he didn't just stand there and ask if I was okay. He scooped me up in his arms and carried me home. (Well, he carried me to his car and then into my house.)

And my dad never really cared about money. He made plenty of it and we lived in a nice big house, but that wasn't important to him. He always said he'd be happy living in a cardboard box as long as he had his four girls—me and my mom and my sisters. Willoughby's family is pretty well off, but it doesn't bother him that I live in a tiny apartment and can't buy brand-name stuff. I think he likes my vintage thrift-store style better than the designer-prep look that's so popular with the Pemberley set. Of course, we don't have much room for personal expression with the whole uniform thing, but there are still subtle ways to insert your personal style.

Most of all, Willoughby reminds me of my dad because Willoughby knows exactly how to make me laugh. I haven't been this happy in a really long time.

And I know that Willoughby and I haven't known each other for very long, but when I'm with him, I can be myself. I can be that happy girl I used to be before everything fell apart. I can forget for a little while about all the horrible things that have happened to me and my family in the past two years.

I think that's what my dad would want. He would want me to be happy. Of course I wish there was some way I could bring him back, but since I can't do that, I have to learn how to keep on living without him here.

I was cleaning my room earlier and I found this poem I wrote right after he died. It's still hard for me to think about that time.

Speechless

What do you do when you run out of words?
"It'll be okay."
All I ever wanted—

The dusty shelves of hoarded childhood trinkets,
The collected ashes of yesterday,
My one bright shining bauble, that last and only thing:
One more speech from you.
"He's in a better place."
I want to hear you yell at me for staying out too late.
I want your whisper in my ear to wake me up for school.
Now I'll only hear you speak in my dreams.
"At least he's no longer in pain."
But you'll never give me that speech.
You won't cheer my name when I graduate.
You won't toast to more years at my wedding.
You'll never repeat all the family gossip.
You'll be forever speechless.
"This will pass. You'll see."
And without your voice, I'm left with nothing but words:
"It'll be okay."
"He's in a better place."
"At least he's no longer in pain."
"This will pass. You'll see."
Just words.
All I want is your words.
All I have are theirs.

I know that poem isn't very good. I could probably make it better if I tried. But it hurts to think about the way I was feeling then, so I haven't bothered to rewrite it.

I think that if my dad could give me one more speech, he'd say something like this, "Keep dreaming. Laugh hard. Love with your whole heart and don't be afraid to make mistakes. Be kind and try your best. I love you."

I love you too, Dad.

Forever and ever,

Vivian

9:30 p.m.

♥ Nila ♥

Dear, darling Taylor,

Everything is going exactly according to my plan. Priyam and Elton came over tonight, and Elton showed us the photo of Priyam that he'd framed. It was pretty impressive, which I probably shouldn't say about a photo that I took. Hahaha.

My dad agreed that it was a nice photo but he said that Priyam was probably freezing the whole time she was posing, which is ridiculous because it wasn't even that cold out last Saturday. Maybe I should've given her my jacket. But that would've thrown off her whole look.

Anyway, I really, really, really hope that Elton asks Priyam to go to the back-to-school dance with him. They would be so cute together!

Maybe I could try to drop hints to him somehow. I did mention the dance when they were both here tonight. Now all I have to do is keep bringing it up until he finally works up the courage to ask her.

Speaking of which, I wonder if anyone will ask me to the dance. I've been so busy lately trying to get Elton to go out with Priyam that I haven't even bothered to check out all the guys at Donwell. The only ones I really know well are Elton and Amar, and I'm definitely not going to get asked by either of them.

Of course, there's no way my dad will let me actually go to the dance. But still, it would be kind of nice to be asked. Oh well. Honestly, none of the Donwell guys are that good-looking. Maybe I'll just wait until college to start dating. That's what Anjali did. And she always seemed perfectly happy with her high school social life.

What about you? Have you met any cute boys in London? What am I saying? How could they not be cute with their accents and their suave European ways?

Please text me soon and tell me you're madly in love with a duke or a knight or something! One of us should have an exciting love life.

Your bffffff,

Nila

FOURTEEN

SATURDAY, 9/17

11:30 a.m.

Vivian

Dear Diary,

Willoughby is being secretive. It's so cute!

We're on our way to his aunt's house and he said he has a surprise for me when we get there, but he won't tell me what it is. I keep trying to trick him into telling me, but so far nothing is working. I'll write again when I have more to report.

Love,

Vivian

12:30 p.m.

Cate

It's Saturday and I decided that today I was going to get out of this house, out of the suburbs, and out into the countryside. It's entirely too beautiful a day to waste the whole thing indoors. When I asked Mr. and Mrs. Allen if they wanted to come with me, they looked at me like I was crazy. I don't think they're really the outdoorsy type.

Then I texted Bella to see if she wanted to come, but she said she's going into the city to go shopping with her sisters and that I should really come with them, since Bella will need my opinion before she can buy anything. I almost said I'd go, but then I looked outside again at the sunshine and how the Bay is sparkling and there's a breeze that's making the trees sway and that settled it. I knew I needed to be outside, and just the thought of spending my whole day in a big city like San Francisco was stifling. You know those days when you just need some real wilderness? Well, today is one of those days.

So then I thought I'd have to go by myself, and I was trying to figure out how to convince Mr. and Mrs. Allen to let me go wandering around alone. And in the meantime I was consoling myself by sitting on a bench in our very, very small front yard. There's only room for the bench, a tiny patch of grass, some rosemary and lavender, and a palm tree. Our backyard is small too—there isn't even any grass there. It's just a big deck with bamboo growing along the back fence. I can't get over how little space there is here compared to all the open land at home.

Anyway, it was already the middle of the morning, and I was sitting out in our front yard and all of a sudden I saw Henry Tilney drive past with Eleanor. So I jumped up and waved to them. I don't know what made me do it, but I was in a desperate mood. Luckily they had their windows down and could hear me, otherwise I would've been making a fool of myself. Henry stopped the car and then they backed up to say hi to me.

We talked for a few minutes, and I told them how I was planning to spend the whole day outside. They said that sounded like a great idea. Then Eleanor asked if she could join me. I had to admit that I didn't actually have any plans. That's when they said they had been planning to go for a long bike ride. I don't have a bike, but they said that was okay, that they could go hiking instead and I should come with them. And now they've gone home to change while I get ready. This is going to be amazing!

1:00 p.m.

Anne

I've just spent an hour with Frederick. Just the two of us. Oh, it was awkward.

I don't even know where to start.

Maybe I should go back to my last entry and tell you everything that's happened since then.

So on Tuesday the Musgroves had their big backyard barbecue, and I didn't really talk to Mr. Wentworth much because we were sitting at opposite ends of the table. And since it was the Musgroves, it was a really long table with at least fifteen people on each side. Honestly, their barbecues are massive. They invite the whole neighborhood.

It was still a little weird to see him talking to Louisa, especially since I know how she feels about him, but it was fine. I mean, I got used to it by the end of the night.

Then the next night he came over to the Musgroves again, and I happened to be there, helping a few of the younger Musgrove kids with their homework. I do that sometimes. They're cute kids and the occasional tutoring session with them keeps me from forgetting everything I ever learned about geometry and chemistry.

So I was at the kitchen table with the kids, and Mr. Wentworth was playing a game with Louisa and Henrietta and Charles and Mary in the living room, so once again we were in the same vicinity without actually having to interact. And I started to wonder if this was how it was going to be from now on. I'd get to be just close enough to him to not be able to forget him, but just far enough away to make it impossible to be friends with him. Not to mention anything more than friends. (Which I'm not mentioning. Ever. Because I know he's forgotten me and moved on with his life, as any sane, rational adult would.)

Ahem. Where was I? So we kept seeing each other in passing, but we still hadn't had a conversation until this morning.

Because here's what happened. Today's Saturday, and Mary and Charles had some errands they needed to run, so I offered to stay here with the boys. Things were going fine until Louisa and Henrietta showed up. They were just stopping by to see how Walter was. He's doing really well, by the way—almost completely recovered.

After checking on us, Louisa and Hen left to go shopping. They wanted me to come with them. They always seem to want my opinion on the clothes they buy. I don't know why. I guess they think I dress well.

Little do they know, dressing well was sort of a requirement for me when I was growing up. Have I mentioned my dad before? And how obsessed he is with looks?

It was like he was running his own personal version of *What Not to Wear* with me and my sisters. He never let us step out of the house without inspecting our outfits.

So anyway, they wanted me to come with them but I couldn't leave the boys by themselves and I wasn't going to try to drag two young boys around the mall to look at clothes, even though Louisa was sure that the three of us would be able to handle them.

About an hour after they left, I decided to let the boys watch TV while I graded some papers. Oh, and I should probably mention that I was in sweats and an old T-shirt. I still hadn't showered. And I wasn't wearing any makeup. It's Saturday. That's how I roll.

And that's the exact moment when Frederick decided to knock on the door.

Walter answered the door and then yelled for me that there was some guy there. I came walking in from the kitchen, and there he was. He looked amazing. He always does. I hate my life.

I think I said something like hi and asked him what he was doing there.

He said he was supposed to meet Louisa and Henrietta here and then they were going out to lunch.

I told him they weren't back from their shopping trip yet.

He said he was sure they'd be back soon.

And then there was a long pause. A really long pause.

Finally I asked if he wanted to come in and wait. I tried not to do it. I really didn't want to spend any more time with him while I was looking like such a mess, but I couldn't help it. He was just standing there, not leaving.

He said yes, he'd like to wait. So he came in and sat with me in the kitchen where I was grading. That was when it got really awkward. Not because anything happened. Because nothing happened. And neither of us seemed able to say anything. It was like I suddenly realized exactly how long eight years is. I'm not even sure if he's the same person I used to know. I can't remember what we used to talk about. And the only things I do remember are too painful to bring up now.

It's not like we weren't trying. We both made little efforts to carry on a polite conversation, but everything fizzled after only a few seconds. It was bad.

Finally, I gave up on grading and went to check on the boys. Frederick came too.

The boys' show was just ending and of course they wanted to watch another one, but I try to limit how much TV I let them watch because if I didn't, they'd stay on the couch all day.

I'm not sure if it was a strong desire to escape the awkward nonconversation we'd been having in the kitchen or if Frederick really is this cool, but all of a sudden, he just stepped in. The second I turned off the TV, he asked the boys if they wanted to play outside with him. And then he spent the next forty-five minutes chasing my nephews around the backyard while I watched from the back deck and tried to get some more grading done.

And why is it that men are so attractive when they're good with kids? It's awful. It might be the single most bewitching trait in the history of mankind.

Thank goodness Henrietta and Louisa finally made it back from the mall before my ovaries exploded.

When they all finally left and Charles and Mary came back, I went back to my apartment to recover. And that's where I am now.

Still in my pajamas. Still hopelessly attracted to Frederick Wentworth. And more sure than ever that nothing will ever come of it.

Please excuse me while I scream into my pillow.

—A.E.

2:00 p.m.

Cate

It's so beautiful here! Henry drove us to Briones Regional Park. He and Eleanor have been here lots of times, but of course I never have. We hiked up a trail to this little pond. There wasn't much water this time of year, but I still think it looked beautiful. Then we kept hiking until we made it to the top of this huge hill. You can see for miles and miles up here. It looks like a place only vampires would visit. The meadow grasses have all died in the summer drought, so instead of being green like the grass is at home, this place is a brilliant golden color. Sort of like a hayfield right before you harvest it.

The trees here are awesome. They have these cool twisting branches. Eleanor said they're Spanish oaks. They remind me of home, even though we don't have the same kind of trees there. But that earthy smell is almost the same. The sky is a soft white-blue color with some high clouds streaked across it. The world seems so still but also full of promise. I always get that sort of feeling in the fall. Like I can sense the impending change of the season, but I know it's not quite here yet. And then suddenly it is here and the fall is over and all the branches go bare.

I'm so glad I'm here. And I'm so glad Henry and Eleanor are here with me. Right now they're talking about the landscape and taking pictures on their phones. They said they want to come back some time with their real cameras and see if they can get some shots. They know a lot more about photography than I do. It's kind of embarrassing. But they don't seem to care that I have no idea about foregrounds and focuses.

I'm stretched out on a picnic blanket, trying to memorize every sensation I'm having right now, from the smell of the dirt and grass to the feel of the sunshine on my back to the sound of cows lowing in the distance.

In fact, I'm so happy I don't even want to write it down. I'm going to stop writing and just soak it in.

3:00 p.m.

Vivian

Dear Diary,

Well, we made it to Napa, but I still don't know what the surprise is. Maybe he'll tell me during dinner. Oh, one thing I didn't realize before we got here is that Willoughby's aunt is out of town. I assumed I'd get to meet her, but apparently she left on a business trip right before we arrived. Willoughby says she travels a lot for work, but he's allowed to come and go as he pleases and it's not a big deal. I think it's a little strange that we're here when his aunt is gone. I guess it's fine though.

And there's a housekeeper/maid kind of person who lives here all the time, so it's not like Willoughby and I are here alone. I'm sure my mom wouldn't mind, but I might not mention to Alice that his aunt was gone until we get back. Alice has very high morals and she's bound to think the worst of this situation, when really there is nothing going on. I happen to have pretty high morals too, even if I don't project them onto everyone else around me the way Alice does.

Anyway, it's almost time for dinner so I'd better go.

Love from Napa!!

Vivian

4:00 p.m.

♥ Nila ♥

Dear Taylor,

Remember how I told you that Elton and Priyam and I were planning to go to the movies? Well, we were all supposed to go tonight, but then this morning, Priyam texted me to say that she had to stay home and help her auntie with something so she couldn't come. So then I texted Elton to tell him we'd have to do it some other time, but he was like, "Oh, I already bought the tickets. I guess we'll just have to go without her."

That seemed strange to me, and I was about to text

him back, but then I saw Amar out in his yard. So I went over to talk to him for a few minutes and somehow the movie came up. Amar said he'd been wanting to see the new Star Trek movie, so I told him Elton had an extra ticket for that night, and he should come with us. Then he gave me this weird look.

And then this happened.

Him: "Are you inviting me on your date with Elton?"

Me: "No! What? It's not a date! It was supposed to be me and Elton and Priyam, but now she can't go, so it's just the two of us going to the movie as friends."

Him: "It sounds like a date."

Me: "Well, it's not. And it definitely won't be if you come with us."

Him: "Yeah, but actually, I think he might want it to be a date, even if you don't."

Me: "Um. No. In case you haven't noticed, Elton does not like me. He likes . . . someone else."

Him: "You mean Priyam?"

Me: "I refuse to comment on my friends' love lives."

Him: "Nila, he doesn't like her."

Me: "Yes, he does. And besides, there's no way you could know about it. Have you spent any time with them? No."

Him: "Not with them together. But I know what he's like. I know what his type is, and you—well, it's not Priyam."

Me: "And I think you're wrong. Besides, sometimes people can't help who they fall for. Priyam is super sweet, and she's beautiful and smart. Why shouldn't he like her?"

Him: "Look, I know you like her. And, yeah, she's sort of pretty but she's just not that cool, you know? Elton is all about his popularity."

I mean, seriously, what do you even say to that? Priyam's only "sort of pretty"? And she's "not that cool"? Who does Amar think he is? It's not like he ever dates anyone. How would he know about this stuff? And who cares about being popular, anyway?

So finally I said, "Priyam might not be popular, but she's still my friend, okay? You shouldn't insult her."

Him: "I wasn't trying to insult Priyam. I was just stating the facts."

Me: "You're a jerk, you know that?"

Him: "Wow, Nila. You're so mature."

And that's when I decided to leave. But as I was walking back to my house, he yelled out, "What time is the movie?"

And I said, "It doesn't matter. You're uninvited, jerk."

So now I'm in a fight with Amar and I have to go to this stupid Star Trek movie with Elton in like fifteen minutes. And I keep hearing Amar's voice in my head saying things like, "It sounds like a date."

Sometimes he makes me so mad.

Hope you're having a better day than I am.

Love,

Nila

FIFTEEN

SUNDAY, 9/18

11:00 a.m.

♥ Nila ♥

Dear Taylor,

I hate it when Amar is right!!!

This is so frustrating, I don't even want to write it down.

First of all, I was wrong about Elton—he is a total jerk. When he picked me up to go to the movie, he didn't even seem to care that Priyam couldn't come. That should've been my first clue.

Then after the movie was over, he drove me home, and then . . . he tried to kiss me!

I know!

I was so mad. He obviously got confused or something, and I told him that. But then he was like, "I'm not confused. I like you."

Uh . . . what!?

I didn't really have a response to that, so I just marched into my house.

But now he keeps texting me, wanting to know when he can see me again and if I'm mad at him and what's going on.

I haven't responded. And I'm not going to.

How could he like me? He likes Priyam. Doesn't he know that? It's been obvious to me for weeks now.

I'm hoping this whole thing will just blow over. I really think he must've gotten confused somehow. I don't know how he could've gotten the idea that I . . . That we . . .

Whatever. I refuse to spend another minute wasting my time thinking about him. He's already ruined my night. Why should I let him ruin my whole weekend?

Okay. Whew. Sorry, I just had to get that out of my system. Anyway, how are you? Have you done any more sightseeing lately? Where else have you been in Europe? Have you made it to the south of France yet? I can't believe I've taken so many years of French lessons and never been to Paris or Africa or French Polynesia or any of the other cool and exotic places where they speak French. You are so lucky to have a family who travels—even if it means you're thousands of miles away from me during my time of crisis.

Anyway, I hope you're having a wonderful time. I love you. And I'm sorry I ranted.

Your best-best friend forever and ever,

Nila

1:00 p.m.

Lizzie

I have news. Last week my dad got an email from one of our neighbors down the street, Mrs. Collins. We have never gotten along with the Collins family. They're the kind of neighbors who file a complaint with the homeowner's association if your Christmas decorations aren't up to par.

Anyway, apparently Mrs. Collins emailed my dad to see if their son could stay with us while they're out of the country. Why she emailed my dad, I have no idea. I mean, first of all, why would they pick us for him to stay with out of all the neighbors they have? There are four teenage girls in this house. Five if you count Jane, which you should. She's still here all the time. We can't possibly be the best choice. Plus, why email? And why my dad? He barely knows Mrs. Collins. They could've just stopped by to talk to my mom. She's here all the time.

Whatever. The point is, they did email. And my dad, being my dad, said yes.

I love my dad, but he has no idea what kind of misery he's about to inflict on the rest of us. He's the kind of person who will see this whole thing as a giant joke. In fact, I think he finds Junior Collins amusing in, like, a crazy reality TV show kind of way. I actually don't know Junior Collins's name, so I think I'll call him JC from now on.

Ew. I hate that I'll need to call him anything. But I guess since he'll be staying *in our house* for weeks (!) he's bound to come up in my journal a few times.

Ugh.

And not only is he staying with us, but he's staying in *my* room! The room that was supposed to be all mine now that Jane has gone to school! The only good thing about Collins staying there is that half of the walls are still covered in Jane's unicorn wallpaper. Hahahahaha.

Serves him right.

But sadly, this means I'm stuck bunking with Mary for as long as he's here.

Sigh.

Mary's room smells.

5:00 p.m.

ALICE-

Today I miss my dad. I try not to dwell on it most of the time because I know it won't change anything, but some days are really hard. I miss how he used to take care of me and my mom and my sisters. I miss how happy our family used to be.

When he got home from work, we'd all run to meet him, especially Amy. She'd start yelling the minute she heard the garage door open. And he always had some little treat for her, even if it was just a penny or a piece of gum or something.

He was so good at knowing when I needed him. When something's bothering me, I don't always like to talk about it, but I like to know that I don't have to deal with it alone. My dad would never try to force me to talk, the way my mom does sometimes. He would just bring his laptop into my room after dinner and sit at my desk while I did my homework on the floor or on my bed. That way he was there if I felt like talking. But most of the time, we just worked together in silence. I miss having him do that.

He was so good at fixing things. If he noticed that something was wrong or that someone needed help, he never waited to be told what to do; he just jumped in and did it. It didn't matter if it was something little like unloading the dishwasher or something big like a car that broke down on the side of the freeway. He was always jumping in to help. My mom says I'm like that too and that I get it from him. I guess she's right. But it was a lot easier to jump in and fix things when he was here to do it with me. Now sometimes I feel like I'm the only person holding my family together.

I just can't believe he's gone forever. It's been so long since I got to talk to him. I wish I had someone who really understood me like he did. He was a serious person and our grades were really important to him, so if we weren't doing well in school or if we were being disrespectful, he would ground us from TV or going out with our friends.

But he definitely had a soft side too. Every so often around bedtime, he would start a pillow fight with me or one of my sisters. It always took us completely by surprise. And then pretty soon the whole family would join in and we'd all be laughing and screaming together.

I know Vivian misses that about him too. Amy's a little more resilient. I think it helps that she's younger. But I catch her looking at old pictures on our computer sometimes. I worry about her. I'm not sure how she'll do, growing up without our dad. I owe so much of who I am to him. I just hope Amy can remember enough about him to keep her grounded.

Vivian should be home from Napa in an hour or two. I hope she had a good time. It was quiet around here without her.

6:00 p.m.

FIONA

It's Sunday night and I'm going crazy. I do NOT want to go to school tomorrow. I keep finding these annoying notes everywhere. I'm sick of it.

I wish I could just do online high school or something. That way I could learn everything I need to know without having to actually talk to anyone.

William called me today. He asked if everything was okay without Dad here. I told him things were fine. I don't want to worry him. But things are not fine. Everything's spiraling out of control. I even got a B- on my math test on Friday. I always get As. I don't know what's wrong with me, but this never happened when my dad was here.

Tonight everyone else went to the Crawfords for dinner, but I stayed here because I was still talking to William when they were leaving. He sounds like he's having fun in college, so at least one of us is happy. He also said he's planning to come visit me at Christmastime. My dad's coming home for Christmas too. I'm excited to have both of them here.

I really don't know why I write in this journal. It's so stupid. It's not like writing things down ever changes anything. My life is still just as horrible when I stop writing each time as it was when I started. Except now I have a record of how crappy everything is.

Maybe I could ask Ms. Elliot if she'd let me do an alternate assignment or something. I'm starting to hate writing in here.

Whatever. She won't let me, so there's no point in even asking.

I really hope those notes aren't from Jack Crawford. He has to know I would NEVER go to a school dance with him. I mean, that should just be obvious to him.

He's a flirt and a horrible person and I do NOT like him. I'm sure he knows that.

Unless he really can't take a hint.

Like, at all.

7:00 p.m.

Vivian

Dear Diary,

We're on our way back to my house. I just realized I forgot to write about Willoughby's surprise. It wasn't as big of a deal as I thought it was going to be. The surprise was that he cooked me dinner at his aunt's house. And it was really, really nice of him. He's a surprisingly good cook. But I don't know. I guess I was sort of hoping that he would make things a little more official. I know I feel like his girlfriend, but he's never actually called me that. And I've never told him that I love him, even though I do and I'm sure he knows it. But he's never said it to me either, so I can't be completely sure that he loves me back, even though I think he does. It's like we're both waiting for the other person to make a move.

The only thing I can really be one hundred percent certain about is how I feel about Willoughby. So let me just state it here for the record: I am completely in love with Austen Willoughby. I know that we're young, but I can't imagine being with anyone else—like ever. If he asked me to marry him right now, I'd say yes. Some people would say that's crazy, but I don't care. I've never cared what other people think. Willoughby is everything I want in a man. He's funny and sweet and so easy to have a conversation with. He's actually interested in things like art and music and books.

And he's so romantic!

Like last week when he came over for dinner, I was complaining about how tiny our apartment is. My mom agreed with me and said she was hoping we'd be able to move into a bigger one next year after our lease is up.

But Willoughby said, "No! You can't move!"

Then my mom said, "Oh, we'd still be in Kensington. We'd find something close by."

"No. I love these little apartments. If I could, I'd move our family into the one next door."

And then Alice said, "Why would you want to do that? Your parents' house is so nice."

It is nice. I haven't spent much time there because Willoughby would rather we hang out at my place or go out together. But he really does have an awesome house.

Anyway, Alice said to Willoughby, "You're telling me you'd trade a house with three stories and a view of the Golden Gate bridge for a tiny 1,000-square foot apartment with narrow hallways and a kitchen with a broken vent?"

And he just said, "Yes. I've been so happy here. My parents' house is big but it's boring and quiet. Every time

I come here, I have fun and I get to see Vivian. I love this place."

Okay, I would keep writing, but I'd rather be talking *to* my awesome boyfriend instead of talking *about* him. And yes, I did just call him my boyfriend. We may not have said it out loud yet, but I don't care. That's how I think of him, so that's what I'm going to call him—at least in this diary.

Love from a boyfriend-having,

Vivian

PS—Napa was beautiful. I hope Willoughby takes me there again someday.

SIXTEEN

MONDAY, 9/19

3:00 p.m.

Cate

I'm undecided about something.

So there's this dance coming up, the back-to-school dance. And Bella thinks it would be awesome if we got our brothers to come home from Mansfield for it and take us. I was kind of hoping to go with Henry.

Not that I'm expecting him to ask me or anything, although that would be totally awesome if he did. But I figured maybe I could just go in a group with him and with Eleanor and whoever else they're planning to go with?

I don't know. I hadn't gotten that far in my fantasy.

And I haven't talked to Eleanor about it yet because I wanted to resolve this thing with Bella first. But Bella is kind of insisting that I bring her and John and James.

They actually can't come if they're not part of my group since I'm the only one of us who is a student at Pemberley.

I don't know what to do. I can't imagine this ever happening to one of the girls in the books I read. They're usually more concerned about escaping from werewolves than they are about who to go to a dance with.

And, yes, I realize it's only one dance and it's really not that big of a deal, but it is my first official high school dance, and I'd kinda like to make it count.

At least Mrs. Allen's got me covered as far as my dress. We went shopping yesterday and picked something out together. It's really pretty. It's short and yellow so it's kind of summery, but it's lacy on the skirt and I think it's perfect. Mrs. Allen thinks so too. She's even lending me a necklace to wear.

Wow. If I stay here much longer, I'm totally going to turn into a girly-girl. My brothers will think it's hilarious. I spent my entire childhood reading books and playing sports outside.

In fact, I'm not sure I've ever worn a dress before now. Well, except for that one Christmas party when I was eight. But I've tried to block that entire episode from my memory.

Trust me, journal. You do not want to know about that.

Let's just say that between the bowl of grape punch I spilled in the kitchen and the hay fight my cousins started around the manger, my dress did not survive the evening. My mom still gets mad at me when someone brings up that party.

Maybe I should call my mom and ask her what I should do about this dance. I know what she would say, though. She would tell me to make a pro/con list. Or two.

Pros and Cons of Going with Bella

Pros:

- Get to see James
- I wouldn't have to plan anything. Bella would take care of all of it
- I'd always have someone to talk to
- Things wouldn't be awkward (unless I get stuck with John all night the way I did when we visited Mansfield)
- I think I'd have fun
- Bella really is one of my best friends and I should be nice and let her come to the dance if that's what she wants to do

Cons:

- I'd have to go find Henry once I got to the dance
- What if Henry asks someone else to go to the dance?
- John really does bug me
- It's just not what I had in mind

Pros and Cons of (Trying to) Go with Eleanor/Henry

Pros:

- I'd get to spend the whole night with Henry
- Henry would be way more likely to ask me to dance with him
- I could invite Eleanor over here so we could get ready together (Apparently that's a thing girls do. Or so Mrs. Allen tells me.)
- I'd have a reason to talk to Henry for the next couple of weeks while we're making plans

Cons:

- It'd be super nerve-wracking
- Am I really sure they'd want me to go with them? I don't want to intrude if they don't want me around
- I don't know if Henry's even planning to go. I assume he is, but I don't know it for a fact or anything
- Bella would probably be really mad at me

Darn. I think it's decided—I'm going with Bella and James and John. Oh well. I'm sure there will be other dances. And I'll probably still see Henry there.

TUESDAY, 9/20

4:00 p.m.

Lizzie

Oh, it's bad. It's worse than bad. It's horrific.

JC has moved in. And he is CREEEEPY!!!

Yesterday I caught him staring at me from down the hallway, but it was one of those things where I was looking in a mirror and I saw him looking at me, but then when I turned around, he ducked out of view. I'm telling you, living with this guy is like being in a horror film.

I cannot believe my dad agreed to this.

The only person in our house who seems to be enjoying having him here is Mary. But I'm guessing that's just because she's no longer the weirdest person under our roof. Actually, my mom seems kind of immune to him too. Probably because he keeps complimenting her on her decorating choices.

He's such a suck-up.

And he keeps checking me out.

Yeah.

Makes me throw up in my mouth a little every time.

Remind me to ask Wickham if JC is this gross at Donwell. Wait, why would Wickham and I want to talk about JC? Why would anyone ever want to talk about JC?

5:00 p.m.

♥ Nila ♥

Dear Taylor,

I have an idea. Why don't I come visit you in London for a while? I would love to see you, obviously. And I could really, really, really use a break from everything going on here.

Of course I'm kidding.

My dad would never let me go to the grocery store alone, much less fly to London. He's so terrified of flying he'd probably make me take a boat to get there. And as much as I would love to miss that much school, I'm already falling behind in a couple of my classes and that would only make things worse.

So what's going on that I so desperately need to escape from? . . . I don't want to talk about it. Let's just say this. Priyam is miserable, now that I told her about Elton liking me. And as much as I keep telling her to get over him because he's so not worth being miserable about, she's still heartbroken, and every time I see how upset she is, it only makes me feel worse because I'm the one who talked her into liking him in the first place.

Elton himself is only making things worse. Now that he's finally gotten it into his skull that I don't actually like him—AT ALL—he's gotten all revenge-y online. I don't know if you've noticed, but he keeps posting these passive-aggressive comments that are supposed to be cryptic but totally aren't. Like for the shots I posted of that photo shoot we did with Priyam, he commented, "Girls are so stupid . . . especially a certain one." So pathetic.

And I only picked that comment to share with you because the others are even more rude. I finally had to block him yesterday because it was getting way out of hand. But Priyam can't bring herself to unfriend him yet so she's still seeing all this stuff.

And now he's started flirting online with this girl from Maple Grove High. It's all super public and super annoying. And this girl looks like total trash. But you didn't hear that from me.

All I'm saying is, I wish I could make it all go away. Not just for me, but for Priyam. She deserves a better friend than I've been to her. And she definitely deserves a better guy than Elton. I can't believe I thought he was worth her time.

I just can't figure out who to set her up with next. I'll have to keep working on it. At least it will give me something to do that doesn't involve listening to

Amar gloat about how wrong I was about Elton. Why are all guys such idiots?

Okay, rant over. I love you. I miss you. Come back to me!!!

Love,

Nila

PS—I wish I'd listened to Amar when he tried to warn me about Elton, but you can NEVER EVER tell him I said that. EVER.

7:00 p.m.

Lizzie

Eww!!!!!!! Ew. Ew. Blech and also ew.

JC just asked me if I'd go with him to the school dance. At the dinner table. In front of my entire family. And my mom said yes for me.

Oh. My. Gosh.

I'm so furious. I can't even.

I'll have to finish writing this later. The only thing I want to do right now is go for the world's longest walk and get as far away from my house as possible.

Maybe if karma is extra kind to me, JC will come looking for me, and then when he's out walking he'll get hit by a car or something.

That would be awesome.

Please, please, karma. Please let that happen!

8:00 p.m.

Anne

Well, Louisa and Fred are on a date tonight. And I am . . . happy for them. Really. I am.

I am very happy. They are both wonderful people and they obviously like each other. So that's just peachy.

Am I convincing you yet?

I don't even want to talk about it.

Instead let's talk about school. All of my classes are going pretty well. The girls seem to be enjoying this journaling assignment, for the most part. Some of them write more than others, but that's to be expected.

We're due to start reading *Romeo and Juliet* next week. That's always fun with classes full of hormonal girls. I can't wait for the inevitable debate on whether or not Juliet should've faked her own death.

Personally, I always thought she should've gone for Benvolio. He's so much less drama than Romeo. But I suppose he's still a Montague, so it wouldn't have made much difference.

This isn't working. I need a better distraction. I know. I'll go visit Mrs. Russell. Wish me luck forgetting my woes!

—A.E.

SEVENTEEN

WEDNESDAY, 9/21

2:00 p.m.

Vivian

Dear Diary,

Guess what! Something amazing has happened! I have a piano! And it's a really nice one too!!! At first, when my mom started telling me about it, I assumed it was a super romantic present from Willoughby because he knows how much I love music. Turns out it's not—it's from our old neighbors the Brandons—but I'm still really excited about it. I went over to their house to see it yesterday and kind of test it out before they moved it over here and it was sooooo nice. The sound quality is amazing, for one thing, and it's a white baby grand.

Alice keeps worrying that it won't fit inside our apartment, but my mom said we'll take out the couch if we have to. I love my mom!

While I was there, Niall Brandon came and talked to me as I was playing. He's really quiet, but he seems nice. We've known the Brandons forever, but I've never spent much time with Niall. I wish Alice liked him. I think they'd be perfect together. Not that he seems interested in her or anything, but they're both quiet and good students and they're both seniors, so it would make sense. Unfortunately, Alice is still too hung up on Peter to do anything about it, and Brandon is not the type of guy to act without encouragement.

Oh well. Right now I'm just in raptures about this gorgeous instrument that's about to become all mine! Neither of my sisters play as well as I do. Not to brag or anything—it's just a fact. And neither of them really care that much about a new piano, but for me this is a really, really, really big deal.

I'm at school right now, but I can't wait to get home to play it. It's supposed to be totally moved in and tuned and everything by the time I get home. I can't believe the Brandons are being this generous. They know how much I love to play and how I haven't been able to play at home since we moved because we had to sell all our old stuff to help pay the bills. They are so kind and generous! Today is a great day! I can't stop smiling!

Love from a super-happy,

Vivian

3:00 p.m.

FIONA

The mystery of the notes continues. So far the message is: Will you go to the back-to-school dance with . . . But it's obvious by now what the question is. What's not so obvious to me is who is sending these notes and if this is for real or just some kind of cruel practical joke that my stepsisters are playing on me. I'm hoping the person sending them will end this whole thing by revealing himself (or herself). Until then, I'm determined not to make a fool out of myself by assuming that they're real.

People like me don't get asked to dances. Not like this, anyway. If I got asked to a dance it would be as a last-second replacement for someone who found something better to do, and I'd get asked in a text or a Facebook message or something lame like that.

Besides, I'm 86 percent sure Edmund is not the one sending these notes, in spite of the fact that multiple notes have now made it past my front door and into my bedroom.

He's not acting any different, and I know Edmund well enough that he wouldn't be able to hide something like this. He's not sneaky. If he were up to something, I'd know it.

So anyway, if it's not Edmund, then it's either a joke or it's from someone I don't like. Someone like Jack Crawford. I SO hope these notes aren't from him, but I'm starting to suspect that they are. He really is the kind of guy who would ask me out as a practical joke.

I just wish I could talk to Edmund about this. I haven't told anyone about it yet.

The best thing to do when people are teasing you is to refuse to acknowledge it and hope they get tired of not getting a reaction out of you.

So that's what I'm going to do with these notes.

5:00 p.m.

Cate

The dance is in three days, and I still don't even know if Henry's going. I wanted to ask Eleanor about it during gym class, but we're doing water polo now and it's kind of hard to have a casual conversation with someone when you're underwater.

By the way, I'm starting to think this school is a bit over the top. I mean, I knew when I applied for my scholarship that Pemberley was a private school with "an illustrious history" per their website, but seriously . . . water polo? In a regular gym class? Next thing you know we'll all be going horseback riding on the school's resident herd of horses. I'm just saying—this place is a bit . . . posh. Is that the right word? I've only heard it used on BBC. Which we only watched because my dad is addicted to *Top Gear.*

Anyway, what with water polo and then awkward showers in the locker room, PE hasn't seemed like the best time to ask Eleanor if her brother is coming to the dance. She's probably already realized that I like him, but I really don't need our entire PE class finding out about my crush. I do try to have a little dignity, you know? Well, in public. In this journal, I pretty much just say whatever I want and assume that my English teacher won't bother reading my journal because she'll find more interesting things to read in other people's journals.

I'm definitely not the most interesting person at this school. Some of these girls have real, live boyfriends, after all.

Okay. Just because I'm bored . . .

Top Ten Most Interesting People at Pemberley

(or in other words, girls whose journals I'd most like to read)

1. Eleanor Tilney—Okay, fine. She's not actually the most interesting person at school. She's normal like me. But I personally would love to read her journal because she lives with Henry Tilney. See how that works?
2. Alice Du—She's the school president. She's involved in everything. And she seems pretty cool. Plus if there are any political scandals going on here at Pemberley, she'd be bound to know about them.
3. Caroline Bingley—Head cheerleader. Major drama queen. I'm sure she has interesting things to say about all of us. Assuming she actually writes in her journal and doesn't just make one of her lackeys do it for her.
4. Mary Crawford—I know everyone's big on Caroline, but I think Mary's prettier in a quirky sort of way. And she's definitely a partyer. She would have lots to talk about.
5. Nila Suresh—She's hilarious. I don't know her very well because she's only a freshman, but she cracks me up every time I talk to her. Okay, all two times I've talked to her.
6. Mary Bennet—She is really out there. Like majorly weird. I don't know, what can I say? I've always had

a thing for outsiders. Maybe it's because I know what it's like to be one. I was homeschooled after all. And Mary's right in the middle of a bunch of sisters. Even if *she's* not interesting, she would know all the family gossip.

7. Bella Thorpe—Doesn't count because she doesn't go to Pemberley. But I really do wonder sometimes what she thinks of me. Mm . . . Yep. That's all I'm gonna say about that right now.
8. Charlotte Lucas—I've read a few of her blog entries and she strikes me as being pretty cool. And like, normal and down-to-earth. Which is more than you can say for her best friend, Lizzie Bennet. Not that Lizzie is crazy or anything, but . . .
9. Lizzie Bennet—see above.
10. Lucy Ying—Something is up with that girl. She's into everyone's business and she's kind of obsessed with Alice Du in particular. I don't know what her thing is, but I'm mildly curious. I wouldn't give her the satisfaction of asking her about her secrets out loud. But if I had a chance to peek into her journal, I'd take it. That's all I'm saying.

Well, that was a waste of time. I still don't know what to do about Henry and the dance. If I saw him more often it might be easier to figure out, but I don't and even though I have his number, we haven't really broken the texting barrier. I mean, I could text him if I really needed something, but we don't just text out of the blue. So . . . ?

Oh well. I'm sure I'll figure it out eventually.

7:00 p.m.

Anne

When I was eighteen I thought I knew what I wanted out of life. I wanted to get far away from this little town. I wanted to move out of my dad's house. I wanted to travel. I was up for adventure.

What happened to that girl? I'm only twenty-eight. But I feel so middle-aged. I've finished college. I've got a great job that I love. I've got a nice boyfriend, even if he does live on the other side of the planet. For the most part, I'm happy as I am. I don't even want to travel anymore. It sounds like too much of a headache to be worth it. Plus it's expensive and I'd have to figure out time off from work. Even in the summer during our school break, it just doesn't sound that appealing. Maybe that's something that comes with age.

But sometimes I wonder if I live like this because I really enjoy it or because it's my routine. Every day I do the same things. I get up and shower. I go to work. I teach. I grade papers. I come home and do my dishes or I hang out with Mary and her kids or go visit Mrs. Russell. I have a few friends, but not many.

Maybe it's time for me to make a change. I don't know what it is yet, but I know it's coming. I talked to my dad on the phone today. He and Elizabeth are fine. They still love their new condo and how close they are to the beach. Actually all he wanted to talk about was all the celebrity sightings he's had lately. He's so weird. I think he thinks the celebrities are stalking him instead of the other way around. It's a good thing he has no idea how to work a camera—even on his cell phone—because I could totally see him becoming a paparazzo.

I'm thinking about going to visit them over the holidays. I know I should. It's been too long since I saw them. But whenever I visit, I remember all the reasons I didn't move with them in the first place. We're just very, very different.

Mrs. Russell says I'm more like my mom than the rest of my family is. I wish I'd had more time with my mom. It's strange that I've now lived almost as long without her as I did with her.

I don't know why I'm in such a sentimental mood today. Maybe that's another thing that comes with age.

Nothing new to report about Mr. Wentworth and Louisa.

—A.E.

EIGHTEEN

THURSDAY, 9/22

2:00 p.m.

FIONA

The notes really are from Jack.
I can't believe him! It has to be a joke.
I don't know what to do.
I hate my life.

4:00 p.m.

♥ *Nila* ♥

Dear Taylor,

Well, I knew this day would come. I just always imagined that you'd be here for it. I am officially going to my first high school dance. Can you believe it? I thought there was no way I'd be able to go because of my dad. You know how he gets. If it were up to him we'd spend every night at home together, watching reruns of medical documentaries and drinking herbal tea.

But Amar and his parents came over last night and somehow with all four of us working together, we

convinced my dad that I should be able to go out every once in a while for special occasions, like a high school dance.

The funny thing is, I don't even want to go, really. Sure, it will be nice to get out and dance with my friends, but Priyam's not going because she says she can't face seeing Elton there with his new girlfriend. Oh, did I mention she's his girlfriend now? Facebook official and everything. Blech. Whatever.

I told Priyam she should just come anyway. Like she should take the high road, you know? But she completely refuses. And it's not like I'm dying to go and see Elton there either. I know Amar is going, but I'm assuming he'll do his usual thing that he does at dances and spend the whole night hiding in a corner with his buddies, not dancing with anyone. I'm sure there will be some other people there that I'll know, but really, I just wish you were still here. If you were, we could go together and it would be so much fun. Now I'll be forced to spend the whole dance with Kira Cole and her friends, who all think I'm stuck up just because we go to the country club. I can't help it that my dad has a lot of money. It's not like I asked to be born into a rich family. It's just the way things are, and I can't do anything about it.

I'm sorry. I don't want these letters to be just me complaining all the time. So I'm going to try to come up with something positive to say about this dance. Okay . . . well . . . um . . .

Hey, at least it's an excuse to buy a new dress. Priyam said she'd come shopping with me tomorrow, so that will

be fun. And maybe if I try hard enough I'll be able to talk her into coming with me to the dance. I really think she should. It's not like we'll even have to talk to Elton. Besides, she has to get over him sooner or later and she's seriously driving me nuts—so my vote is sooner, not later.

Okay, wish me luck with these positive thoughts. Let's have a Skype dance party soon to make up for the fact that you're not here to go to this dance with me.

Hope you're having a great week! Love you lots!

Nila

5:00 p.m.

Lizzie

I still have no words. There's no way to describe what my life has become. JC has been living with us for four days and it feels like he is everywhere. He takes the world's longest showers. He always seems to be right outside my bedroom door. He gargles his cereal milk. It's disgusting. Is it possible that all boys are this creepy and gross? I know I've lived with girls my entire life, but JC must be an exception of some sort. I can't imagine Liam Darcy, for example, picking his toenails at the dinner table.

And it's not just that. It's the snivelly suck-uppy-ness. He's so simpery and whiny all the time. He's like a little shell of a person, so fragile that you're tempted to toss him out a window just to see if he'll float away on the wind or fall flat to the ground and splinter into a thousand pieces.

Ew. I can't believe I'm waxing poetic over JC's ego of all things.

In other news, I am *not* going to the dance with JC, thank goodness. I went for that walk after leaving the dinner table, and I walked for probably two hours and then it got really dark, and I realized I needed to go home. And when I got back, my dad was waiting for me out on our front porch and he said he'd talked it over with Mom and he only wanted me to go to the dance with JC if I wanted to.

So I told my dad that I definitely didn't want to. And he said that was fine and he'd handle it. It was actually really sweet of him. I love my dad.

I know my mom only wants the best for me. She thinks that having a boyfriend and going to dances is part of the quintessential high school experience and she doesn't want me to miss out on anything. Plus, like I said, I think she's kind of immune to JC's creepiness for some reason. But I don't see why I can't just go to the dance with my friends.

What ever happened to that big group of girls I used to hang out with all the time? Now every single one of them—except Charlotte—has a date to the dance. Why do we have to drag guys into everything? We're only in high school. Can't I just have fun with my friends? All I want to do is hang out with Charlotte and get my groove on. If it were up to me, I wouldn't invite any guys at all. Well, except maybe for Wickham. I ran into him at the grocery store the other day, and he's still just as hot as I remembered. Maybe even hotter. I keep hoping he'll ask me out, but so far nothing.

Well, at least I still have my bestie. Charlotte and I are going to have a blast as each other's dates!

Later

7:00 p.m.

Charlotte is going to the dance with JC. Apparently when I said no, he went straight to her house and asked her. I can't believe this is happening. I can't even talk about this right now. I just needed to write it down.

FRIDAY, 9/23

6:00 p.m.

FIONA

The dance is tomorrow night and I don't want to go to the dance with Jack. Even if he really is asking me and it's not a joke.

But it is a joke. It has to be, right? Why would he ask me? We're not even friends. And he knows I don't like him. He could've asked Julia. Even Mariah would've been a better choice, and she has a boyfriend.

He flirts with both of them all the time.

It doesn't make any sense that he would ask me. Is there any possibility he got confused or thought he was sending the messages to someone else in my house? But the notes had my name on them. I just don't get it.

I really want talk to Edmund about it. But what's super scary to me is that Edmund might already know. He might be in on it. I don't know what to think anymore. But if I find out that Edmund has started to make fun of me too, even just behind my back, I will lose it. I need at least one person in my life who's not constantly trying to laugh at me. Is that too much to ask?

I can't trust anyone right now, and that is the worst feeling.

It's time for dinner, but ever since my dad left, my stepmom doesn't really care if I come down for dinner or not. I told her I wasn't feeling well tonight, and I'm glad I did because I heard the Crawfords come in a few minutes ago. I didn't even know they were invited.

I hope we have enough food for them. I made lasagna tonight. Whatever. If there's not enough, they'll just have to deal with it. I can't be expected to make enough food for the Crawfords if I don't know they're coming.

Anyway, now I'm just holed up here, in my attic, with only my homework to comfort me. It's a good thing I like school so much. I even like math. Or maybe I only like it because it's the one thing in my life that has always made sense.

I don't understand my family. I barely have any friends. I don't know how to talk to people, and I definitely don't know how to spend hours in the bathroom putting on makeup and making sure my hair looks perfect—nor would I want to know how, frankly.

But I do know how to learn and how to get good grades. So maybe I'm not completely hopeless. Now all I have to do is figure out how to survive until college. Do you think I could stay locked up in my room that whole time? It's only another two and a half years. And I think Edmund would bring me some food to keep me alive.

I have a bathroom.

I could make it.

SATURDAY, 9/24

Cate

It's 3:48 am. I couldn't sleep, so I started reading, and now I just finished the last book in this vampire series. And that's when it hit me.

Are you ready for this?

What if Henry is a vampire?

No. Listen.

The evidence has been right in front of me this whole time. I should've seen it.

1. He's super handsome.
2. He disappears for weeks at a time.
3. He won't talk about his family. I have no idea where his mom is or if he even has one.
4. His sister is also sort of standoffish, but in a nice way.
5. He's a gentleman. He has good manners. Like maybe he's from another era.
6. He dresses well and he's charming. Everyone likes him.
7. He's rich.
8. He just moved here from out of town.
9. From what Eleanor has told me, their vacation house on the Lost Coast is basically a haunted castle.

The list goes on. All I'm saying is, it's worth further investigation.

NINETEEN

10:00 a.m.

ALICE-

The dance is tonight and I am so busy. Vivian is going with Willoughby, and she's really excited about it. We went dress shopping a few nights ago. My mom and Amy came too and it was fun. Probably the most fun we've had as a family since my dad died.

Is it weird that I'm excited for this dance? I'm not even going with anyone, but I have to be there as senior class president. Somehow, I still think it's going to be fun.

Well, fun and a lot of work. But that's fine. I always feel better at a social function if I have some sort of task that I'm in charge of. And maybe that will help keep my mind off the fact that I don't have a date and there won't even be anyone there that I want to dance with. Peter's not really the dancing type. And even if he was, he wouldn't ask me to dance with him.

That's just the way it is, and I accept that, and I'm fine with it. Life goes on. And now I should probably go get ready. I've got lots of work still to do. Wish me luck!

11:00 a.m.

FIONA

My life is so screwed up. My stepmom and I are in a huge fight and everyone in my "family" is mad at me. Even Edmund.

Last night when the Crawfords came over for dinner and I was hiding up here in my room, Jack told my older stepbrother Tom about the notes he'd been leaving me. I think Jack was probably just trying to find out if I was planning to answer him. (I wasn't.)

But Tom who is here for the weekend—again!—thought the whole thing was hilarious, and he ended up telling everyone right after the Crawfords left. Julia and Mariah were furious. They completely freaked out. As soon as they found out, they ran up here to my attic and forced me to come downstairs and tell them what was going on.

They kept asking me all of these questions like how long I'd been dating Jack and why he even agreed to go out with me. I tried to tell them that we weren't dating, that I don't even like Jack, and that I don't *want* to go out with him. But they refused to believe me.

And their mom took their side, of course. She said I must've been sneaking around with him for weeks. She won't even let me explain anything. She just thinks I'm—in Julia's words—"a boyfriend-stealer." Which is really unfair because Jack's not even going out with either of them, and Mariah actually *has* a boyfriend. A fact that so many people around here tend to forget/ignore. Poor Rushworth.

This whole thing just makes no sense at all.

Anyway, when I wouldn't admit to being anything, my stepmom got mad and said I was grounded, so that takes care of my problem, actually. Now I can't go to the dance with Jack, because I can't go out at all. So everything is great.

Except that I'm stuck here in a house with five people who all hate me.

Okay, Edmund doesn't hate me, but he's not happy with me. He came up here to talk to me late last night. He was really annoyed that I wouldn't just go to the dance with Jack. But he doesn't get it. I can't pretend to like someone when I really don't like that person. And furthermore, I'm still convinced Jack doesn't like me at all and that this was just part of some elaborate scheme like out of one of those '80s high school movies.

Edmund doesn't think so. He thinks Jack actually likes me, but he doesn't get it. The Crawfords are completely fake. He just can't see it because he has such a huge crush on Mary. I think he only wanted me to go with Jack so that Mary would come with him and we could be like a cute foursome. I can't tell you how much fun that would *not* have been.

The only good news I have to report is that Mary's not going with Edmund. She's going with Tom. Edmund told me the whole story. Last night at dinner Mary kept flirting with Tom. I think she was just trying to make Edmund jealous. But then Mariah told Tom that he should take Mary to the dance and she said yes! Mary has no shame.

Edmund told me he was planning to ask her after dinner. He was just really nervous about it. I feel bad for him, but I'm so glad he and Mary won't be going together. Maybe this will show him what a horrible person she is.

I just want to curl up in a ball on my bed and not move for the next twenty-seven hours, at least. I hate my family. I hate the Crawfords. I hate high school. I hate life.

11:30 a.m.

Cate

Well, it's morning. Real morning now. Like 11:30 a.m. And after getting some sleep, I'm not as convinced that my crush is supernatural. But I have to say, I'm not totally unconvinced either. Is that crazy?

I just think that he's mysterious. There's something about him and his family that they're not telling people. I don't know what it is, but I'm going to find out somehow. And their vacation house? Or castle or whatever? I need to get inside that place.

Eleanor told me all about it once. It's called Northanger Abbey. That alone is enough to creep some people out. But on top of that it's super old and tons of people have died there. Mostly just from old age, but still. I have to go see it sometime. If I consider myself an expert on vampires, witchcraft, and all things paranormal—which I do—I owe it to myself to visit this place and find out what's really going on with these Tilneys.

2:00 p.m.

Vivian

Dear Diary,

Oh my gosh! I can't believe it's finally here! It's the day of the dance!!! I am so, so, so excited.

Alice and I picked out the most gorgeous dress for me to wear and I'm going to do my hair up and paint my nails to match my dress and it's going to be awesome! This is the best day ever!

Of course, Alice is already freaking out. She has her "calm" face on, which is always a bad sign. I guess there was some mix-up with the caterers or the band? I'm not really sure, but she's on the phone with them now. I can't believe how much work goes into putting on one small dance.

But I'm grateful that Alice does it all because she loves that sort of thing, and I definitely wouldn't want to be in charge of something this big.

Anyway, I need to go get in the shower. I only have six hours until I'm supposed to meet Willoughby in front of the school, and I have to look absolutely perfect. Tonight is our big night. We'll be making our debut as a couple in front of everyone—all his school friends and mine. I want us to look like we belong together. Because we do. I know we do. I love him, and I'm so excited to dance with him. It's going to be completely magical!

Love from an enchanted,

Vivian

3:00 p.m.

Lizzie

I'm still in shock. I can't believe Charlotte is going to the dance with JC. She's a senior. He's a freshman. Plus he's . . . he's . . . awful. And icky. And gross. I just want to barf every time I think about him. And now who am I supposed to go with? I can't go by myself. That'd be totally lame.

I really wanted to go too. I know it's just a high school dance and there will be more of them, and it's not like this one dance is going to be anything special, but I was really hoping to see Wickham and all my friends there, and even my little sisters are going. I have a dress and everything. Yeah, I know—me in a dress.

Sigh. I don't know what to do. The dance is tonight and I have two tickets because I bought Charlotte's for her before I found out that she was going with JC. I should go, I guess, but I really wanted to go with Charlotte and now . . . gah! How could she do this to me?

Later

4:00 p.m.

Okay, this might sound crazy, but I think the problem is solved. Jane just showed up at home to help us all get ready, and my mom told Jane that she should go to the dance. I could tell Jane was about to say no, but then she looked at me, and I must've had my super-pathetic sad face on because she agreed to come with me.

My beautiful, self-sacrificing sister is now my beautiful,

self-sacrificing date to the first high school dance of the year, even though she's already in college. I love her. I love her for doing this for me. And I love her for acting like this is what she was hoping for all along.

Actually it's not like it's unprecedented. I mean, I can guarantee Jane won't be the only Mansfield student there. A lot of people who used to go to Pemberley and Donwell come back for the dances. It's not like there's much else going on for people our age around here.

In fact, I'm pretty sure Bingley will be there too.

Huh.

Maybe that's why Jane agreed. This is all making a lot more sense now.

Well, regardless of her motives, I'm glad Jane is going. We're going to have a blast.

And now I really do have to get ready so I don't look like a total mess. After all, I wouldn't want to disappoint my "date."

TWENTY

5:00 p.m.

Anne

Ben called me. He wants me to come visit him. I told him I'd have to think about it. I haven't told him yet about Mr. Wentworth. Not that there's anything to tell. I mean, Fred and Louisa are pretty much together now or about to be or something, so I don't think I should feel guilty about not telling my boyfriend that there's a guy here teaching at my school that I used to . . . whatever.

I do feel bad about keeping something from Ben. We've never had secrets before. And I know all about his romantic history. He was engaged once, to a girl from his hometown. But then she died in a car accident a few months before their wedding. It scarred him pretty bad. We met a year or so after that. I think I was the first person he opened up to about it. And he's still good friends with her family—the Harvilles. I met them once when we visited Ben's hometown.

Anyway, the point is, I know so much about him, and he knows so little about me. Don't you think that's weird?

Maybe I should see if he wants to come here instead.

Then he can at least get to know my life a little better. I feel like he knows me as a person, but he doesn't know what I do every day and all the stuff I care about here. It would be nice to have him meet Mary's kids.

And, okay, I'll admit it. It would be nice to have my boyfriend or whatever he is here when I have to see Louisa and Mr. Wentworth together. Ben would be a nice distraction.

I know it's stupid, but I still feel a little insecure about this whole situation. I think it's great that Louisa and Mr. Wentworth are dating, but there's a small part of me that can't help but feel like he traded me in for a newer, younger, better-looking model of girlfriend.

Which is ridiculous. I'm the one that broke up with him because he wasn't good enough. That's not what I thought, of course. But my dad and Elizabeth and even Mrs. Russell felt like he wasn't worth my time and that I shouldn't get tied down when I was so young. We were in high school and we were talking about getting married. It was too much. I couldn't handle the pressure from my family.

Right before we left for different colleges, I told him it was over. And then I never heard from him again.

I thought it was over. It took me a long time, but I thought I was over him.

So I hate that I'm having these thoughts now. I like Louisa. I want to be happy for her. And obviously Mr. Wentworth and I could never get back together. He would never forgive me for what I did. So I should want him to move on. And I do. It's just . . .

I would rather he didn't move on right here, where I can see the whole thing. And maybe not with my sister's sister-in-law.

I have to stop writing now. I need to get ready. I'm chaperoning the dance tonight and I'm sure Mr. Wentworth and Louisa will be there too.

Time to go put on a happy face.

—A.E.

7:00 p.m.

♥ Nila ♥

Dear Taylor,

This will have to be just a quick note because Amar will be here any minute. He's giving me a ride to the dance. I wish you were here to see me. I look awesome. Hahaha. I know I shouldn't say that about myself, but it's kind of true. Anjali came home for the weekend to do my hair and help me get ready. She's such a sweet older sister. And it's so nice to have her here. Most of the time she's too busy with her research projects at Mansfield to come home. My dad was elated when she walked in the door.

Anyway, I'm actually really excited now. My dad has been taking pictures nonstop. I'll post some soon so you can see for yourself how hot I look. Just kidding. Sort of.

I don't know why I'm so giddy. It's not like anything's going to happen at this dance. It'll be all the same people I see at school and around town every day. But it feels different. Special. I can't help wishing that something wonderful might happen. You just never know.

At the very least, I'm hoping I spot someone new to set Priyam up with. She could really use someone in her life to keep her from thinking about Elton's new girlfriend.

I'd better stop writing so I can do one last mirror check. Because if I have to meet Elton's girlfriend tonight—which I will—I really need to look especially awesome. And I'm also going to have to pretend to like her. Ugh.

Oh well. I will not let Augusta Hawkins ruin my first high school dance.

I will not. I will not. I will not.

Love you,

Nila

PS—I think Augusta is such an ugly name.

7:30 p.m.

Cate

Bella is here. I'm supposed to be putting on my makeup with her, but I swear we have spent the last four hours putting on our makeup. I had no idea it was even possible for a girl to use so many different powders and creams all at once.

Mrs. Allen is really into it too. She keeps offering to help us with our dresses or get us water or do another quick facial mask for good measure. It's like a beauty salon threw up in the guest bathroom. And the smells! There are lotions and hair sprays and I don't even know what else, and every single one has a different scent.

I'm going crazy.

Okay. I think we're actually ready to go

downstairs, which is good because the guys got here half an hour ago and John Thorpe has been ranting about us being late for at least twenty of those thirty minutes. I don't know why he cares. He's never been on time for anything, according to Bella. I think he's just bored.

Oh goody. That means it will be up to me to keep him entertained all evening so he doesn't get crabby and try to leave at 9:30. Bella will kill me if she has to leave early. She wants everything tonight to be perfect. I don't know why it's *my* responsibility to keep *her* brother happy, but she is my best friend, I guess, so what are you gonna do?

In other news, I have confirmation that Henry will be at the dance. Eleanor too. Yesterday she mentioned something about her dress for the dance to one of the other girls in our PE class, so I asked her if she was going and she said yes and that Henry was coming too. Isn't that awesome?

I just have to keep reminding myself during all this chaos that it will all be worth it when I get to dance with my super handsome (possibly vampiric) would-be boyfriend.

Heh. I have to stop calling Henry a vampire. If I keep doing it, pretty soon I'll start to believe it. But he isn't. Because that's crazy.

He isn't.

Right?

8:00 p.m.

ALICE-

So far everything is going smoothly. I sorted out the caterers and then there was a minor debacle with the DJ's equipment, but everything is fine now and people are starting to arrive.

I think this is going to be okay. Most of the people here look like they're enjoying themselves. I'm cautiously optimistic that this night is going to be a success.

That's a relief. If it all goes well, I might be able to talk Vice Principal Norris into giving us a bigger budget for our next school dance. Ticket sales for this dance were really high, and if I can make dances popular this year, it should help us to fund some important projects I've got planned.

But I'm getting ahead of myself. Time to stop writing about all this and focus on making sure everyone has a good time.

8:10 p.m.

Peter is here. I saw him talking to Lucy in the corner, but just for a minute. I could tell he didn't want anyone to notice them. He hasn't talked to me at all yet, but he waved when he came in and seemed happy to see me.

Niall Brandon asked if he could put his name down on my dance card. He's a nice guy. It's too bad we're not interested in each other. It would definitely be convenient. Much more convenient than liking Peter, who I'll never get to be with.

But it doesn't matter because Brandon doesn't like me. And I don't like him.

8:15 p.m.

Anne

I love Pemberley. It's such a quirky, old-fashioned school. I can't believe they still use actual dance cards at their dances. I think they brought that tradition back a few years before my older sister started coming here. It's pretty cute. All of the boys have to reserve dances with the girls by writing down their names on the girls' cards. It's sweet. Awkward, obviously. But sweet.

Plus, it's fun to see the kids all dressed up. I'm stationed at the check-in table, where there's enough light to see everyone in their dresses and suits and sparkly shoes. They all look so happy. Totally carefree. I hope this dance and these years are everything that they should be for my students.

Sometimes when I see them, I can't help but remember what I was like in high school. My mom was so sick. And then after she passed, I wasn't the same. I wanted to be happy, but I felt like I'd already left childhood behind.

I wonder how many of my students feel that way. I've been glancing at some of their journals (only the ones who gave me permission, of course) and it's been really eye-opening. Some of them are dealing with a lot. I should give them more credit, I guess. I know what that's like.

Of course, being here is also bringing back some memories of the last dance I went to in high school. I went with Frederick, of course. And we were so completely wrapped up in each other back then.

He's here with Louisa. They came in a few minutes ago. This is the first dance he's been to at Pemberly since that one we went to together. I wonder if he's doing the flashback thing like I am. Probably not. I'm sure he's much too emotionally evolved for that.

I'm the one who can't let go of the past.

—A.E.

TWENTY-ONE

8:30 p.m.

FIONA

This is so unfair!

I got a text from my brother this afternoon, saying he wanted to Skype with me tonight, but I can't because my stepmom took away my laptop when I got grounded. I can't believe the one time my brother is actually available, I'm not allowed to see him. She even took my phone away once everyone left for the dance.

Now it's just me and my stepmom at home. I think she's watching *Hoarders* downstairs. She loves that show. It makes her feel superior. She's such a snob.

This sucks. It's been so long since I got to talk to Will. If my dad were here, he'd let me use Skype.

I didn't even break any rules. This punishment makes no sense. Most people get grounded for going out with someone. But not me. I get grounded for *not* going out with someone I didn't even like in the first place. Or was I grounded because I got asked out? I don't even know anymore. It's so stupid.

9:00 p.m.

Lizzie

I can't believe it! Wickham's not even here! I got all dressed up, and for what? It's not like I care about looking good for Darcy. This dance is the worst.

At least Jane's having a good time. She's danced with Bingley twice already.

I'm so annoyed. I was really hoping I'd get to see Wickham again. And Lydia said he was coming. She sort of Facebook stalked him and that's how she found out he was planning to come. I told her I couldn't condone her methods, but I was still hoping she was right.

Some guy I don't even know asked me to dance. He introduced himself while we were dancing, but I can't remember his name now.

But now I'm stuck here in a corner, next to the refreshments, with no one to talk to and no one to hang out with. Charlotte keeps trying to get me to come over to her group, but I refuse. If I'm going to be miserable at this dance—and apparently I am—I'd rather do it alone than with JC.

Oh! Which reminds me! This was probably my favorite moment of the night so far. It was awesomely hilarious.

When JC came in, he spotted Darcy right away. I was standing with Jane, who was standing next to Bingley, who was standing next to Caroline, who was standing next to Darcy, so I got to watch this whole thing happen.

JC looked like he was fidgeting for a minute or two, and then he came straight over to Darcy and stuck out his hand for a handshake.

JC: Mr. Darcy, I'm so pleased to see you here.

Liam: Who are you?

JC: My name is Collins. We attend Donwell High together and my parents work on the city council with your aunt.

Liam: Okay.

JC: Well, I just wanted to introduce myself properly. I've seen you around school, of course, but never in such a suitably informal setting.

Liam: Uh . . .

JC: I wonder if you would allow me to say how grateful I am for the work your aunt is doing. I know that her projects are of vital importance to our local economy, and I so admire that entrepreneurial spirit that is at the heart of all our city's small businesses.

Liam: What are you talking about?

JC: I just think it's wonderful that your family is so involved in the community. It must give you lots of influence over our local government.

Liam: Okay, I really don't know who you are or why you're talking to me, but I'm gonna go.

And then he just backed away. It was priceless. And JC was, like, crushed. You would've thought from his face that Darcy was one of his heroes. Who knows? Maybe he is.

Sadly, aside from that bit of merriment, this dance has been a total disaster.

I'm going back to my lonely post at the punch table. Fun times.

9:30 p.m.

Vivian

Dear Diary,

It's almost nine-thirty. The dance started over an hour ago. I'm starting to get really worried.

Willoughby said we should meet in the parking lot in front of the school and I haven't seen him yet. Alice came out to check on me a few minutes ago. I told her Willoughby had just texted me and that he was on his way, but that's not true. He hasn't texted me. I haven't heard from him at all. I don't want to assume the worst, but I'm scared. What if something happened to him? What if he got in a car crash or something? I keep trying to call him, but he's not picking up. This is horrible.

I just need to calm down. I'm sure everything's fine and he'll be here any minute now. I'm overreacting. I know I am. Pretty soon he'll show up and we'll laugh at how worried I was and everything will be fine.

It's chilly out here. If Alice comes back, I'm going to see if she'll let me borrow her jacket.

Love from a nervous and slightly freezing,

Vivian

10:00 p.m.

Cate

I can't believe this! John is gone. What in the name of pop rocks is wrong with him?

I wish I hadn't said yes to Bella's plan. Now I'm stuck

here at the dance with her and James, and they're too wrapped up in each other to even notice me.

Yeah. Bella just told me in the girls' room that she's in love with my brother. I had no idea! I mean, I sort of wondered, but I was just guessing. It's one thing to guess and quite another thing to hear it spoken out loud.

This wasn't how my night was supposed to go. I've barely seen Henry. I've been stuck here at this table in the corner, trying to entertain John and now he just left out of the blue while I was in the bathroom. Not that his absence really makes a difference. He wasn't talking to me. He kept messing around on his phone all night. I'm so annoyed.

My dance card is completely empty. Bella and James have danced every single slow dance together, which she is over the moon about, but after one dance with me, John said he was tired and just wanted to sit down.

Well, you know what? If John can ditch me, then I can ditch James and Bella. I don't know how I'll get home, but I'm sure if I really have to, I could call Mr. Allen. I'm sick of sitting here, watching other people have fun. I'm off to find Eleanor and maybe Henry too.

10:15 p.m.

♥ Nila ♥

Dear Taylor,

You will never believe who is here! I still can't believe it myself. I was totally unprepared when he walked into the room. I was just standing next to Amar, who was talking to some of his friends, when all of a sudden I saw him. It was like one of those crazy moments that only happen in dramatic TV shows. The lights were dim, and we were on opposite sides of the room, but instantly I saw him and I knew exactly who it was.

Okay, is the suspense killing you yet?

It was Frank!

I know! Your cousin Frank!

I haven't seen him in ages. He looks good. Like grown up and masculine. Not the way I remembered him from a couple of years ago.

I still haven't had a chance to talk to him so I have no idea what he's doing here at our dance, but it's exciting! I knew something was going to happen tonight. I just knew it.

All right, I'm going in. Wish me luck. Why am I nervous? It's just Frank. But also . . . it's Frank!

Whew. Here goes.

More soon!

Nila

TWENTY-TWO

10:30 p.m.

Lizzie

Uh . . . something weird is happening.

I was just sitting at a table, nibbling on pretzels like a good little loser when all of a sudden I felt like someone was right behind me.

So I turned, and there was Liam Darcy. Like way too close to me. It was kind of freaky. So I stood up to face him and almost tripped in my heels. So embarrassing. But it was his fault for startling me!

Anyway, Liam was like, "Are you missing your dance card?"

And I was like, "Why? Did you find an extra one?"

And then he said, "Oh. No. I just wasn't sure if you had one. I couldn't see it anywhere, and I haven't seen you dancing much so . . . I didn't . . . uh . . . I didn't know."

"Oh," I said. "Um. Well, yeah. I do. I have one."

"Okay. Cool."

Then there was a super long pause of awkwardness. Like really, really long. A banana slug could've made it across the Sahara during this pause.

And then, finally, Liam said, "Can I see your card, then?"

"Huh?"

Yeah. That was my witty response.

"I . . . I want to dance with you," he said.

That's when I knew I must be asleep and that this was all a weird dream. Because there is no way, in any version of reality that Liam Darcy would ask me to dance. I mean, what the . . . ?

But it's been a solid ten minutes since that happened, and his name is still there, written in pen, on my dance card.

What is happening to my life?

11:00 p.m.

Anne

Fred just came over to see if I needed any help at the check-in table. He's all dressed up for the dance, and he looks . . . well, he looks good. Too good for my comfort. I told him I was just about finished since nearly everyone has arrived. Then he said that once I was done, I should join him on the dance floor. I wasn't sure if that meant join him in chaperoning or join him in an actual dance. But right then Louisa came up and said this was her favorite song, so Fred went off and danced with her.

Oh well. I'll let them enjoy themselves.

In the meantime, I'm having fun here at my post. I've just realized that this journaling thing has really caught on with some of my students. In the past ten minutes I've seen at least three girls sequester themselves in odd corners and scribble furiously in their notebooks. I had no idea they'd get so into it.

Of course, I know they've been writing because I've been checking periodically to make sure they're still adding new material. I just didn't know they'd be so dedicated. I mean, bringing your journal to a dance? And sneaking away to write in it. As an English teacher, I'm thrilled.

On the whole, I think it's been good for me too. To write in a journal, I mean. I'm not sure how I would've dealt with this whole re-emergence of Fred in my life without some place to write it all out.

—A.E.

11:05 p.m.

FIONA

This is so boring. I've run out of homework to do. I already practiced my oboe for an hour and a half. It's past 11:00. I'm in my pajamas. I should probably just go to sleep. I wonder when Edmund and everyone will be back from the dance. I want to wait up for them, but I'm tired and there's nothing to do around here.

I actually sort of wish I was out with them.

What the heck? The doorbell just rang. And now my stepmom is yelling for me. What is going on?

11:10 p.m.

Anne

Apparently it did mean dancing with him. What Fred said, I mean. Sorry. I'm a little thrown off right now.

He just came up and asked me to dance straight out. I'm not sure what to think. I said yes, of course. It was a gut reaction. But why did he ask me? There are fifteen chaperones here and he's the only male. It's not like there aren't other people he could dance with. Of course, some of the chaperones are a little elderly. I'm not sure Mrs. Bates could've heard him ask, and she certainly can't dance with her walker, but she's still a perfectly good school librarian.

—A.E.

11:15

FIONA

Oh my gosh! I can't believe this is happening! Just when I thought things couldn't get any worse, guess who showed up to prove me wrong? Jack Crawford. I hate him so much right now. I am in my pajamas. There is no way I'm going down there to talk to him.

11:20 p.m.

Anne

I have to go. I can't stay here. I have to get out of this room. Too much teenage romance in the air, I think. It's starting to rub off on me and give me crazy ideas. I did my duty as a chaperone. I checked people in. I patrolled the dance floor for a little while.

I even danced with Fred.

And now I have to go.

Oh, I just missed a call from Mrs. Russell. I wonder what she's doing at this time of night. Maybe I'll go see her. Maybe she'll be able to talk a little sense into me.

My head is spinning. I can't even write down my thoughts right now. I know I won't want to read them later.

—A.E.

11:25 p.m.

♥ Nila ♥

Dear Taylor,

This is the best dance ever! I am having so much fun with Frank. I wish he went to Donwell instead of Maple Grove. If he did, I'd see him all the time.

You know how we sort of went out for a few weeks when we were in sixth grade? Well, he's still just as cute as he was then. He's funny and a good dancer. I have no idea why I broke up with him. Maybe the timing was just off. We were really young. How long can you expect middle school relationships to last, really?

But now that we're older, maybe things would be different.

Anyway, I found out why he came to our dance. Apparently your uncle Richard got a free ticket because he's on the Pemberley School Board, so he gave the ticket

to Frank. Frank almost didn't come because he knew you wouldn't be here and he doesn't know very many other people at our school. But I'm so glad he did come. We are having a blast.

The only thing that could possibly make it better is if you were here to enjoy it with us. I still feel bad that Priyam didn't come, but it's nice to not have to worry about how she'll react to seeing Elton and Augusta. Priyam is wonderful, of course, but she's been so down lately that I'd forgotten how much fun it could be to just party with my friends without all that negative energy. I'm so glad Amar convinced my dad to let me come.

I totally forgot how hilarious Frank is. We've been hanging out all night, commenting on people's outfits and the awkward moments going on around us. At one point, Frank was doing a play-by-play sportscaster-type commentary of Liam Darcy asking Lizzie Bennet to dance. I think he might have a thing for her. He's been staring at her all night. Frank noticed it too. Anyway, I'm gonna get back to the dance. I just wanted you to know that your cousin is awesome, and I'm having a really, really great time at my first high school dance.

I love you!

Talk to you soon!

Nila

11:30 p.m.

FIONA

I hate my stepmom. And Jack. She forced me to come downstairs and sit there with her and Jack, and then mid-conversation, she got up and left me there alone with him.

So then he started going on and on about how he really does like me, and why wouldn't I believe him, and how cute I looked in my PJs—totally false, by the way. I checked in the mirror when I came back upstairs. I look like crap.

Anyway, Jack wouldn't leave until I promised to go out on a date with him. He is insane. We have nothing in common. And besides that, he's a horrible flirt. I can't stand him. He doesn't care about anyone but himself. And somehow he's managed to charm my entire family into siding with him, which is totally unfair because I'm the one who's related to them. I mean, shouldn't they be on my side here? But no. Everyone's all, "Jack's so great! Why won't you just give him a chance! You're being so stupid and stubborn."

The worst part is having Edmund be on Jack's side. I thought at least he'd understand.

I get that Jack is attractive and that most girls would be completely flattered by a guy like him asking them out, but I am not most girls. I don't feel that way about him, and I refuse to pretend that I do just for the sake of having a boyfriend. Maybe that makes me a total weirdo, but I'm just trying to do the right thing. Why can't anyone else see that?

I feel like I'm going crazy.

Oh, and as Jack was leaving, he tried to kiss me. I turned my head, so he only kissed my cheek, but it was still completely uncomfortable. How dare he?

I just want to be left alone.

11:40 p.m.

ALICE-

I'm so relieved. The dance is almost over and everything has gone really smoothly. A few minor hiccups here and there, but nothing disastrous. Well, nothing that affects the rest of the student body. Personally, I . . .

Actually, never mind. I came over here to write about this, but it's not going to help.

All that happened was that I saw Peter and Lucy dancing together. But that's it. And that's fine. I mean, it's good. I'm happy for him. For both of them.

If they're willing to take risks like that, then I think that's good. I just hope . . .

I don't know what I hope. I hope he's happy. I'm sure she is. Who wouldn't be happy about dancing with Peter?

Anyway, I should get back to the dance floor. Not that I've been doing much dancing. I've been a little busy trying to coordinate things. And I still haven't seen Vivian in here. Maybe she's avoiding me. She got really defensive when I talked to her in the parking lot earlier. I should probably try to smooth things over. Okay, I'm going to go find her.

I just wish . . .

Oh, forget it. I'm going to focus on a problem I can actually do something about: my sister.

11:45 p.m.

Lizzie

Huh.

I don't even know what to say about this. Liam Darcy and I just danced the last dance of the night together . . . and it was . . . strange?

Super awkward, obviously. And not something I'm ever planning to repeat because not only is he a jerk, but he's also . . .

Well, uh . . .

Hm . . . I'm not explaining this very well.

See, the thing about Darcy is that he thinks everyone is beneath him, and so he just expects people to do whatever he wants them to do.

I just can't figure out why he wanted me to dance with him. And why I said yes.

And why it wasn't the worst three minutes of my life.

I'm not saying I liked it or anything. It was definitely unpleasant. It just wasn't as overwhelmingly awful as I was expecting it to be.

We actually . . . talked. Sort of.

Anyway, whatever. He's still the most annoying person on the planet and completely full of himself and I never want to dance with him again.

I'm going to go find Jane. Maybe with her help, we'll be able to keep Lydia from completely embarrassing herself. The last time I saw her, she was up on some guy's shoulders, chicken-fighting with another girl.

Oh, and speaking of my sisters, guess who made a

surprise appearance here? Mary! Apparently there wasn't much going on online tonight, so she showed up half an hour ago, dressed completely in black and frowning. I haven't seen her since then. She's probably terrorizing anyone who comes into the bathroom, demanding that they wash their hands for a full thirty seconds.

Sigh. Sometimes I can't believe I'm related to these people.

SUNDAY, 9/25

1:30 a.m.

Anne

Well, I'm about to do something completely crazy. I'm quitting my job.

I know. It sounds insane. And I don't know if it's the right decision. I just know I'm doing it.

Wow. I can't believe this is happening. Two hours ago I was at the dance, and now I'm getting ready to leave here, maybe forever. Whoa. That is a scary thought. But also, in a way, exhilarating.

Okay, I need to go pack, but I just want to record this moment. I'm not sure how much longer I'll be keeping this journal, so just in case I stop, I want to remember how this happened and why I'm doing this.

It started when I was dancing with Fred. Well, actually it started a month ago when he showed up at school and burst back into my life.

Anyway, we were dancing tonight and all of a sudden I looked at him, and it was like no time had passed. We were exactly the same people who fell in love with each other all those years ago. And it was amazing. I just wanted to stay there, dancing with him, for the rest of the night.

And then, just as suddenly, the moment was over. The song ended, and we split apart, and that's when I realized that I can't go back. I can't do this to myself again. If I stay here and we work together and I see him all the time, I will fall for him again.

I just can't let that happen. I know he doesn't feel the same way, and I need to be a grown-up about this.

So then I came over here to Mrs. Russell's and she was going on and on about some cheap tickets she found to go visit my dad and Elizabeth this weekend. And then she said she was planning to move there for six months or so, to get out of here before the winter comes.

This was the first I'd heard of her plan, but she was adamant that I come with her. She said I needed to get away and have fun. That I was getting too old too fast and that she'd noticed I hadn't been myself lately. Plus I think she just wanted my company. And she is so hard to say no to. I love her, and that probably makes it even worse for me, but she is seriously the most persuasive woman on the planet.

Obviously the first thing I told her was that I couldn't leave my job, but she reminded me that she's on the board of trustees at Pemberley and she could smooth it over with them. And that's when it hit me. I could do this. I don't have to stay here in this same old town doing the same things I've been doing my whole life. I'm not too old to have an adventure.

And without my job and Mrs. Russell, there's nothing keeping me here.

Well, I guess there's Mary and her family. I'll miss them, of course. But it's not like I can't come back and visit. And I'm only leaving for six months.

After that, who knows? I have no idea what my future holds. A few days ago that thought would have scared me, but now it just makes me excited.

Okay, I really do need to go home and pack. I'll try to remember to keep you posted.

—A.E.

TWENTY-THREE

8:00 a.m.

Lizzie

It's too early to be awake, but my phone just beeped at me. It was Wickham. He texted to say he was sorry about not coming to the dance.

It's weird. I was so mad at him about it last night, and now I'm not sure if I even care. I mean, yeah, it would've been fun to see him there. But I actually think I had a good time, even with all the insanity I had to put up with from my sisters.

And that dance with Liam Darcy?

It . . . uh . . . it wasn't totally terrible. Maybe I've been wrong about him this whole time. Maybe he's not the utterly asinine jerk I always assumed he was. Maybe he's just really, really socially awkward. But instead of coming off as a nerd, he comes off as a snob. A super arrogant, super snotty snob.

It's a possibility, right?

I don't know.

I'm going back to sleep.

10:00 a.m.

Cate

Oh my gosh, I had the best time last night! Once I finally ditched Bella and James and joined the Tilneys' group instead, it was awesome! Their friends are just as cool as they are. They were super nice to me, even though I'd never met most of them before.

And then when the dance was over and it was time to go, I told Eleanor that I didn't have a ride home, and she said Henry could take me. Eleanor had plans to spend the night with her friend Grace, so Henry was just going to drive home alone.

I didn't want her to ask him. I didn't want to be a pain or inconvenience him. They kind of live on the opposite end of town from me, but she insisted that he could take me. So she asked him. And he said yes. And he drove me all the way home to the Allens' house. And then when we got here, we just sat in the car and talked for a while. I thought it was only a few minutes, but then we started getting cold, so he turned the car back on and I realized it had been two hours. It's a good thing the Allens didn't give me a curfew last night. I totally would've missed it.

Finally I told Henry I had to go, and he walked me to my door, and then when we got there, he gave me this little hug. It was cute, but kind of awkward.

I wish I'd kissed him or something. Oh my gosh! I can't believe this is happening. I can't believe I almost kissed Henry last night.

This is so surreal.

I really like him.

12:00 p.m.

Anne

I can't believe this. Everything has fallen into place. I'm really going. I'm leaving here. I'm quitting my job. Actually, I'm not really quitting. I'm just taking a leave of absence. I might even be able to start teaching at Pemberley again if I decide to come back.

That has eased my mind a lot, knowing that I'm not totally throwing away everything I've worked for here. But this is still pretty crazy. Mrs. Russell has bought our plane tickets, rented a townhouse for us, and made sure everything was taken care of. Now all that's left for me to do is pack up my stuff and say good-bye to Mary, Charles, and the boys.

I'm headed over there in a few minutes. I think the Musgroves might be there too. When I called to tell them I was coming, there was a loud ruckus going on in the background, which usually means that Charles's family is there.

That will be good. I can say bye to them all together. I really do owe the Musgroves a lot. They've been so nice to me ever since Mary and Charles got married. They're almost more like my in-laws than hers. In fact, Henrietta told me once that she and Louisa both wish Charles had married me instead of Mary. Isn't that strange?

Well, I'm off to Mary's house. I'll try to write again once we're on the plane.

In only three hours.

This is crazy!

—A.E.

1:00 p.m.

Vivian

Dear Diary,

My life is over. It was a beautifully tragic existence, and now there is no reason for it to continue. Without him, what am I? It was only through his love that I became real, a whole being. I lived for him and through him and with him, and now . . . ?

I was faithful. I spent the entire dance waiting for him to arrive. And not only did I lose my love, I've caught a cold. It's a bitter, dreadful replacement.

He is everything to me. We understand each other in a way I didn't even know was possible. And now that I do know it, I almost wish I didn't because it makes my present pain so much more intense. He opened my eyes to a depth of feeling and my heart to a swelling of love that without him would never have been possible.

And then he took that love and cast it off with so little regard for me that I have to wonder if he is under some mystical influence over which he has no control. How could he do this to me? What have I done? And more importantly, what could I do to win him back?

I know. I will text him again. He must respond sometime. And this text will be so eloquently worded it will show him how I truly feel. Then he'll have no choice but to come dashing gallantly to my side.

And once he sees me here, in tears, my heart breaking more each second, he will feel nothing but agony and he'll assure me it was all a tragic, hapless misunderstanding and that his love for me is constant, unconditional, and completely unwavering. I know it will happen. I know it.

I haven't yet lost faith in him.

Love from a heartbroken,

Vivian

2:00 p.m.

♥ Nila ♥

Dear Taylor,

I'm so tired! The dance was awesome, but exhausting. After it was over, Frank walked me to the parking lot and we talked there for a long time. Then Amar came over and said I needed to go. Frank offered to give me a ride, but Amar insisted that I come home with him. He said he'd promised my dad he'd get me home safely. So that was that. You know how Amar gets sometimes. I don't know what set him off, but he was in one of his moods yesterday. We barely spoke to each other at the dance, and by the time it was over, he was grouchy and tired.

So I got home and went straight to bed. This morning Anjali cooked breakfast and brought it up to me in bed. She wanted to hear everything about my first dance. It's really fun to have her home. I'm not used to talking to her about girl stuff, so it was a little weird at first, but she's actually really cool. For someone who spends all her time in a lab, she knows a lot about boys.

Also, she's convinced that I like Frank and he likes me back. Hahaha. I don't think so. I mean, yes, we had a lot of fun last night. And it's true, I think he's really cute. But it's been so long since I've seen him and I don't even really know him that well. Just because he was my first kiss doesn't mean we're destined to be together. That was so long ago, and we were just kids. In fact, I really don't think it should count as my first kiss. I was twelve. Doesn't your romantic record start when you become a teenager? Although, he was thirteen, so maybe it counts for him and not me? I don't know. Whatever. The point is, I don't think I like him.

Whether or not he likes me . . . ? I'm not so sure about that. And if he did like me, it might change how I feel about him. I'm not sure. I guess what I'm saying is, I could be persuaded. But it would take some effort on his part, and I don't think he's planning to ask me out. So . . . whatever.

But I did have a really fun time at the dance. I'm so glad I got to go!

I miss you! I wish you were here to tell me what to do about Frank and to snap Amar out of his funk. Still not sure what his problem is, but I don't think I care.

Hope you're having a lovely time in London! Say hello to the queen for me!

Yours ever,

Nila

3:00 p.m.

FIONA

I just got off the phone with my dad. He called to talk to my stepmom, but everyone was out shopping. It was so nice to talk to him and to feel like I had him to myself for a little while. I miss him so much. I don't understand why he won't just let me move in with him. I wouldn't mind switching schools. And I wouldn't mind sleeping on a couch or an air mattress or whatever he has in his little apartment. Plus I'd get to experience a whole new culture and maybe even learn a new language. What language do they speak in Antigua? I should've asked my dad.

I just need to get away from here. I hate everyone and everything in my entire life.

Well, I don't hate Edmund. I could never hate him. But I can't believe how much he's changed, even just in the past month or so. He seems obsessed with getting Mary Crawford to like him. So now if she thinks something is right, he automatically agrees with her.

It actually makes me really sad for him. I used to think he was immune to this sort of thing. But apparently he's as bad as any teenager when it comes to liking a girl.

I tried so hard to convince my dad to let me come and live with him. I need to get away from here. I can't take it anymore. All this stuff with Jack is driving me crazy. And I can't stand my stepmom and her glares. She's acting like it's my fault that Jack likes me instead of one of her

daughters. Believe me, if I could get him to go after Julia instead of me, I totally would.

Great. Now I'm crying. I don't know how much more of this I can take. I have no one on my side. I feel completely alone. I have no real friends at school, just people I say hi to. I've started eating lunch alone in the library, hiding my sandwiches from Mrs. Bates because she's a stickler about the no-food-near-the-books policy. I just wish I could curl up in a ball and stay in my bed all day, every day.

Plus, as if my life wasn't hard enough already, I think I'm getting a cold.

I just want to lie here and cry.

At least I'll always have my attic as a refuge. I know no one will come and bother me here.

TWENTY-FOUR

5:00 p.m.

Anne

You will never believe this.

I don't even believe it myself.

You will seriously never believe whom I am sitting next to on the plane.

Okay, let me back up a little bit.

We got to the airport late and had to rush to our gate. Luckily our tickets were for first class seats—Mrs. Russell refuses to travel any other way—so they couldn't get too mad at us. But because we booked late, we couldn't get two seats next to each other. Mrs. Russell took her seat, which is three rows up and all the way on the other side of the plane from mine. I helped her get settled. And then I came back to my seat and saw him.

Sitting in the seat next to mine was a man I never thought I'd see again.

William Walters. My sister's ex-fiancé.

What is it with exes suddenly appearing in my life? I thought I was getting away from this kind of thing by moving to Malibu!

Maybe I should back up again.

My sister Elizabeth dated Will off and on when they were in college, and then right as they were both graduating, he proposed. My dad loved Will. For about a month, everything was perfect. Elizabeth was planning this huge summer wedding. And then right before they sent out their save-the-dates, Will told her he was leaving.

Everyone was shocked and—oh no! He's coming back from the bathroom. I can't keep writing about this. He might see it.

I just can't believe we're sitting next to each other!

—A.E.

6:00 p.m.

Alice-

I think it's time to come clean about something. Well, maybe several things. But first I should mention that Vivian never made it to the dance last night and she hasn't left her room all day. She's just sitting in there, crying. We can all hear her through the walls of this ridiculously small apartment.

Now my mom is pouting because Vivian won't tell her what's wrong. We all know it has something to do with Willoughby, but I can't find out if they had a fight or what's going on. So my mom has spent the entire afternoon lying down in her room with a "headache."

And Amy is mad because we were supposed to go to the zoo today as a family. I offered to take her myself, but she got mad and said she hated me.

I sent her to her room as punishment.

That leaves me, here, alone in the front room, with nothing but my own gloomy thoughts and the occasional audible sob from Vivian as company.

I don't like having this much time to think. I'd rather be working on something.

Times like these are when I start to brood, and today I've been brooding about Peter. I think it might help to write it all down. I've hesitated to write about it in here because as much as I try to keep this journal safe from intruding eyes, I do have two curious sisters and an equally curious mom, and this really isn't my secret to tell.

But I have no one else to talk to about it, and there are days when it really gets to me. Today is one of those days.

But honestly, Ms. Elliot, if you're reading this, I have to ask you to stop. I don't know how much you really read these journals. I imagine with the number of students you have, it would take a long time to read all our journals and you probably have better things to do. I don't really know what you do outside of school, but I'm sure you don't spend all your time working. Anyway, on the off chance that you are reading this, I'm asking you to stop now. Because I promised that I wouldn't tell.

Okay. I'll start at the beginning.

I met Peter Feng the summer before ninth grade. We were both volunteering as junior counselors at an outdoor-ed camp for inner city kids. I knew right away that I liked him. He's quiet like me, but he's more thoughtful than I am. I tend to be really analytical, which makes it easier for me to solve problems. But I think Peter is more sensitive to people in some ways. Anyway, we were able to talk about some pretty deep stuff and after a week or two, I could tell he liked me too. Or at least I thought he did.

As the summer went on, we got closer. But there were times when it seemed like something was bothering him. I just didn't know what it was. That fall we started high school, and I tried to keep in touch with Peter. He didn't always return my texts, so eventually I figured he wasn't interested. But the next year, we started working together on the joint student council and again it seemed like he liked me. At that point, I wasn't sure what to think.

Then I met Lucy Ying. Actually, I had already met her; I just didn't connect her with Peter. Lucy is a grade younger than Peter and me, but she was in my bio class that year. One day while we were working on a lab together, Lucy asked if she could talk to me about something.

She said she knew I was friends with Peter and that he'd said I could be trusted. Then she told me their secret. She said that she and Peter grew up in the same neighborhood and played together as kids. When he was twelve, they realized they liked each other and they became more than just friends.

Then one day Peter's mom caught them kissing—well, Lucy actually said "making out." Peter's mom was furious! She said they were way too young to even think about dating and then she told Peter he wasn't allowed to be friends with Lucy or going out on any dates until he turned eighteen. Peter's mom is super strict and very traditional.

But even though they couldn't see each other, Peter and Lucy wrote love notes. She's actually shown some of them to me. In their notes they agreed to not date anyone else until he turned eighteen and they could be together. Then about a year later, Peter's family moved across town so they weren't even neighbors anymore.

This is why I will never be with Peter. For one thing, he'd have to break his promise to his mom about not dating till he's eighteen. And even if he did that, he'd have to break his promise to Lucy not to date anyone except her. It's never going to happen. Peter's too good to go back on his word.

And since Peter and Lucy have made it this long, I know they'll wait it out until he turns eighteen. His birthday is in March. That's only six months from now.

But even then it will be hard for them. Lucy won't be good enough for Peter's mom. She'll want Peter to date someone rich or famous or both. We live in a really affluent area, and I suppose I understand in a way why money is so important to Peter's mom. She's always buying him new designer clothes and tech gadgets.

The funny thing is, Peter doesn't care about any of that stuff. Ironically, Lucy does, but her family isn't well off so she can't afford to be picky.

I just don't understand why Lucy still likes Peter. They seem so dissimilar to me. She's a cheerleader. He hates sports. She likes to go out and have fun and he'd rather stay home and read a book. He gets really good grades and hers are mediocre at best.

But I guess opposites really must attract because as far

as I know, they are still devoted to each other, even now, years later.

Anyway, I've known about this situation long enough to have made my peace with it. But every once in a while it still stings. Like last night when I saw them dancing together.

It just reminded me of when I first found out. It was awful, especially because I couldn't tell anyone why I was upset. Lucy didn't seem to suspect that I liked Peter at all. She kept asking me for advice about how to get his mom to like her. After awhile Lucy and I became pretty good friends. She seems to think I can fix anything. And I'll admit I like being needed. After all, she would never have passed bio that year without my help.

As for Peter, for a long time I did my best to avoid him. I tried to ignore my feelings and focus on other things. That strategy has worked well. I've gotten good grades. I became student body president. I've done a lot of good things in high school.

I've just never had a boyfriend. Because as much as I hate to admit it, Peter is the only guy I've ever liked. And he is completely and totally off limits.

7:00 p.m.

Lizzie

This has to be some kind of mistake.

Jane got a text this morning from Caroline Bingley that says her brother is no longer interested in seeing Jane. Caroline says that Charles asked her to break the news to Jane. Caroline also said she hopes Jane didn't get the wrong idea. According to Caroline, her brother hangs out with a lot of different girls and he's not serious about any of them, except maybe Gia Darcy, Liam's little sister (who—by the way—is only fourteen). And Charles is a freshman in college. That's just wrong.

What am I talking about? This whole thing is wrong.

So Caroline has to be lying—at least about Gia. Caroline probably thinks that if Charles and Gia get together, Liam will be more likely to become Caroline's boyfriend.

But poor Jane is convinced that Caroline is telling the truth about everything and that Charles never really liked her seriously. To which I said, "Hello? I think the giant teddy bear that's still in your dorm room proves otherwise."

I honestly think Caroline's making this whole thing up and that her brother doesn't even know about it. But Jane has tried calling and texting him a couple of times and he hasn't responded at all. I want to have faith in Charles, but that's not a good sign.

Now Jane's afraid to go back to Mansfield because she doesn't want to run into him on campus and have things be awkward. But that's ridiculous. My mom already agreed to let her stay here tonight and miss school tomorrow because she's so upset, but she can't skip her classes forever.

Speaking of my mom, she is crazy-furious. She can't believe Charles would break up with her baby.

This whole thing just seems so weird. I want to give

Charles the benefit of the doubt, but the longer this goes on, the worse I feel about it. It's like I have this sinking feeling that I should've seen this coming. As much as I wanted to like the guy, I have to admit, he is a Bingley and he is friends with Liam Darcy. I just thought he was better than this.

I don't know what to do now. Why did I think going to the dance would be a good idea? Something must've happened between Charles and Jane there, some misunderstanding. But if he's upset with her, he should at least give her a chance to talk about it.

Ugh. The longer I sit here, writing about it, the angrier I get. I'm going for a walk.

8:00 p.m.

Cate

Whoa! This is amazing! Henry wants me to come with him and his family to visit Northanger Abbey during Thanksgiving break! I can't believe it! I'm dying to see this place. It sounds like it's straight out of a vampire book. I have always wanted to visit someplace haunted and mysterious.

Plus, I'll get to spend two whole weeks there with the Tilneys! This is going to be so cool! I already asked Mr. Allen if I could go, and I called my parents and asked them too. They all said yes and that I should enjoy myself and have a good time. None of them really know the Tilneys, but Mr. Allen has met Mr. Tilney a few times before and he said he's sure they'll take good care of me and that nothing bad will happen to me while I'm there.

Of course, he doesn't know that this place is probably crawling with paranormal energy. Which I think is totally awesome in a thrilling sort of way.

This is going to be so cool! It's like a real adventure from a book or something.

I can't wait!

9:00 p.m.

♥ Nila ♥

My dearest and most lovely and wonderful Taylor,

Today has been a great day. Anjali and I spent all day shopping, which I haven't done in ages. Probably since you were here.

Then she somehow convinced my dad to let us order Chinese for dinner and eat it in front of the TV. He will do anything for her if it means she'll come home more often. It's pretty awesome.

Then when it was time for her to drive back to Mansfield, we all went out to say good-bye to her. Actually, Veer Kulkarni was driving them both back. He came home for the weekend too and they carpooled together. So my dad and I walked Anjali over to the Kulkarnis' house, where Veer was already outside, putting his stuff in the car. And then as they were leaving, Amar and his parents came outside to say good-bye. We all waved to them as they drove down the street.

Then Amar turned to me. I could tell he wanted to talk, but not with our parents around. He asked me what I was doing tonight. I said I was planning to stay home with my dad, but he was welcome to come over and hang out with us.

He kind of hesitated, and right then my phone dinged at me. It was a text from Frank. He said he had so much fun with me last night and that he couldn't wait to see me again and wanted to know what I was doing tomorrow after school. I didn't read it out loud or anything, but I must've smiled or done something to give it away, because then Amar was like, "That's from Frank?"

And I said, "Yeah."

And he said, "Okay. Well, I should go inside."

And I said, "Okay. Maybe I'll see you later then."

And he said, "Actually I have a ton of homework to do tonight."

So I said, "Oh. All right. Bye."

It was weird. Almost like Amar was jealous or something. But that's just silly. I don't know what that was about. But I do know that Frank is hilarious and super cute and I might or might not be going on a date with him tomorrow after school. Even if it's not a date "officially," we're still going to have an awesome time.

It's so weird. I never get this way about a guy. I wonder what Priyam will think. Maybe I should call her. Later. Right now I just want to enjoy this little crush I have and keep it all to myself.

My life is so awesome! I hope yours is too! And I hope

it's not weird for you that I have a crush on your cousin . . . again. But he's seriously so much fun! Of course he is. He's related to *you*!

Okay. Talk to you more soon!

Love,

Nila

EPILOGUE

MONDAY, 9/26

5:00 p.m.

Lizzie

I'm at the park.

This is usually where I end up when I go on one of my frustration walks. It's kind of my spot to have to myself. With four sisters, you don't get a lot of privacy at home, so you have to come up with other places to escape to.

I've never brought my journal here before, but it's nice. I usually just come here to think, but I like being able to write down all the things that are bothering me.

Like:

1. Why didn't Wickham show up at the dance last night?
2. What the crap is going on with Bingley? And why didn't I see it coming?
3. Who is behind this whole thing? Is it Caroline and maybe May, or is it Liam?
4. What can I do to help Jane get over it and get on with her life?
5. What should I do about Charlotte?
6. Why would anyone go to a dance with JC?

7. Did I bomb my history test last week? We still haven't gotten our scores back. I hate teachers that take forever to grade stuff.
8. Where should I apply for college?
9. Did I actually enjoy dancing with Liam Darcy last night?

I'll admit, I thought this whole journal-writing assignment would be stupid when we started it, but it hasn't been that bad. In some ways, it's been really nice. It's like having someone to talk to and bounce ideas off of. I have Jane and Charlotte for that too, of course. But right at this moment, I don't actually have either of them.

Jane is still in our room, crying. And Charlotte . . . who even knows?

I cannot believe she went to the dance with that turtle of a JC. She can't be that desperate for a date, can she? What is the big deal about boys, anyway? So they're cute and you can make out with them—so what? I'd much rather have one really good girl friend than a disgusting date, like JC, to some dance. I would even give up a super-hot guy like Wickham if I had to choose between him and Charlotte.

Apparently that's not how Charlotte feels though.

I hate that it's such a competition at Pemberley. Having a boyfriend automatically makes you cooler, even if the guy you're dating is completely lame. And you can't date outside your coolness range. Like if Liam asked me out, everyone would be shocked because he's that much cooler than me.

Not that Liam would ever ask me out.

And I wouldn't say yes if he did.

This is all hypothetical.

I'm just saying that *if* he did, no one would get it. They'd all think that he was somehow lowering himself to my level. Even when we danced together last night, I could feel the stares.

I'm sure he could too. That's probably why things were so . . . weird.

I mean, I don't know. I didn't hate the feeling of dancing with him. He's actually a really good dancer. He knows how to lead and stuff. You wouldn't think it would matter at a high school dance where you're basically just swaying in a slow circle, but it makes a difference. I wonder if he took dancing lessons or something as a kid. Maybe his dad taught him.

The Darcys are a pretty cool family, actually. I've never spent any time with them, but I saw a bunch of their family pictures on the wall when we were staying at their beach house, and they seem really happy. Plus Mr. and Mrs. Darcy are involved in a lot of community things. Whenever I see the two of them, they look like they're perfectly matched and genuinely happy together.

You don't see that very often. I don't, anyway. My own parents can barely agree on what to have for dinner. I think the only reason they've stayed married is that my dad doesn't have the heart to leave us to fend for ourselves. But he's not happy and neither is my mom. They're just used to being unhappy now.

It's so depressing.

If I ever get married—and as far as I'm concerned,

that's a big *if*—I don't want to do it because it's convenient or because I think it would be easier than being single. I don't want to do it because that's what society expects or because someone really rich is offering to take care of me and my family.

The only reason I ever want to get married is because I'm totally and completely in love with my someone. That way, even if things get hard—and I'm sure they will—we'll always have that love to fall back on.

Sorry. I don't know why I'm rambling on about this.

I'm not planning to get married for years and years. Maybe not even then. I have way too much to do first. Places to travel. College classes to take. Books to read. Discoveries to make.

But I guess I would be lying if I said I never dream about getting married. I mean, it's hard not to think about it sometimes when it's all my mom ever talks about. And who knows, maybe in all of my adventures, I'll meet someone completely irresistible.

Someone as cute as Wickham but someone I can actually count on to show up at dances when I want to see him.

Someone who makes me as happy as Mr. Darcy seems to make Mrs. Darcy.

Someone who is completely the opposite of JC.

Ew! Can you imagine anyone ever marrying JC?! Disgusting.

I don't even want to think about that.

Okay. I have to focus on something positive or I'll never be able to go home and deal with all the drama going on there.

Hm . . .

Hahahahahaha. You should've seen Caroline's face when she saw me dancing with Liam last night!

It was epic. I've never seen someone that mad in real life. I think I've said this before, but it would almost be worth dating Liam to see Caroline's reactions.

Actually, I've spent so much time with Liam lately that I don't think dating him would be completely terrible. At least he'd show up when you needed him. He's always good at being there for his friends. Of course, his personality still leaves a lot to be desired. He's rude and pompous and stuck on himself, but maybe he doesn't mean to be that way. Maybe he's just socially inept. I don't know. The man is a mystery. And I'm not nearly interested enough to try to solve it.

Besides, if Charles Bingley really is out of the picture, I doubt I'll spend much time with Liam. Things will probably just go back to the way they used to be.

Liam will go back to being Mr. Popular—captain of the Donwell soccer team and all-around superstar. And I'll go back to being Lizzie—the secretly amazing girl from a big family who's smart and confident and doesn't care about what other people think.

I like that girl. She's got a good life.

She definitely doesn't need a boyfriend.

Even if Liam is a good dancer.

Who needs the headache, anyway?

I've got enough of that going on already. Speaking of which, I should probably go back home now and check on Jane.

Plus it's getting dark. The sun just set across the Bay a few minutes ago and the streetlights are starting to come on all over Kensington. People are turning on the lights in their houses too. It actually looks pretty cute and cozy.

Want to know a secret? I actually like this little town of mine, especially at this time of night. You can smell the jasmine blooming across from the bench I'm sitting on. And I just watched a family of birds swoop into the eucalyptus tree up the street.

I'm still planning to leave Kensington as soon as I can. But no matter where I go, I know this will always be home. It'll always be the place I come back to and some part of me will always be here.

Whenever I come back for holidays and stuff, this spot in the park will be where I come to think things through.

It's nice to have things like that to count on.

Okay. I really do have to go now.

Ms. Elliot, if you read this, thanks for making us write in journals. So far this assignment hasn't been nearly as cliché as I thought it would be.

CHARACTERS

Dear Readers,

It is with great dismay that I have learned there are still some few of you who have not read all of Jane Austen's novels. For your sake, I hope you will soon remedy that unfortunate situation. But for those who are as yet only familiar with one or two of Miss Austen's works, I now provide the following character guide to link my modern girls and guys with their Austenian originals.

One caveat: I can in no way claim to do justice to these characters. You really must read them in their native books. That way you'll be able to point out all the many ways I mixed them up or got them wrong. I wouldn't want to deny you that pleasure.

And you might even find some clues as to what happens next at Pemberley Prep!

Happy reading,
H. J. D.

Emma

The Woodhouses
Mr. Suresh – Mr. Woodhouse
Anjali Suresh – Isabella Woodhouse Knightley
Nila Suresh – Emma Woodhouse

The Knightleys
Amar Kulkarni – Mr. Knightley
Veer Kulkarni – John Knightley

Taylor Weston – Mrs. Weston
Frank Churchill – Frank Churchill
Priyam Patel – Harriet Smith
Jane Fairfax – Jane Fairfax
Mrs. Bates – Mrs. Bates
Elton – Mr. Elton
Augusta Hawkins – Mrs. Elton
William Cox – Mr. William Cox

Mansfield Park

The Bertrams
Mr. Bertram – Mr. Bertram
Tom Norris – Tom Bertram
Edmund Norris – Edmund Bertram
Mariah Norris – Maria Bertram
Julia Norris – Julia Bertram
Mrs. Norris – Mrs. Norris
William Price-Bertram – William Price
Fiona Price-Bertram – Fanny Price

Mary Crawford – Mary Crawford
Jack Crawford – Henry Crawford
Rushworth – Mr. Rushworth

Northanger Abbey

The Morlands
James Morland – James Morland
Cate Morland – Catherine Morland

The Tilneys
Henry Tilney – Henry Tilney
Eleanor Tilney – Eleanor Tilney

The Thorpes
Mrs. Thorpe – Mrs. Thorpe
John Thorpe – John Thorpe
Bella Thorpe – Isabella Thorpe

Mr. and Mrs. Allen – Mr. and Mrs. Allen

Persuasion

The Elliots
Mr. Elliot – Sir Walter Elliot
Elizabeth Elliot – Elizabeth Elliot
Anne Elliot – Anne Elliot

The Musgroves
Charles Musgrove – Charles Musgrove (father)
Mary Elliot Musgrove – Mary Elliot Musgrove
Charlie Musgrove – Charles Musgrove (son)
Walter Musgrove – Walter Musgrove

Mr. and Mrs. Musgrove (elder)
Henrietta Musgrove – Henrietta Musgrove
Louisa Musgrove – Louisa Musgrove

Mrs. Russell – Lady Russell
Fred Wentworth – Captain Wentworth
Mr. and Mrs. Croft – Captain and Mrs. Croft
Ben Wick – Captain Benwick
The Harvilles – Captain and Mrs. Harville
William Walters – Mr. William Walter Elliot

Pride and Prejudice

The Bennets
Mr. and Mrs. Bennet – Mr. and Mrs. Bennet

Jane Bennet – Jane Bennet
Lizzie Bennet – Elizabeth "Lizzie" Bennet
Mary Bennet – Mary Bennet
Kitty Bennet – Kitty Bennet
Lydia Bennet – Lydia Bennet

The Darcys
Liam Darcy – Mr. Darcy
Gia Darcy – Georgiana Darcy
Anne de Bourgh – Anne de Bourgh

The Bingleys
May Bingley – Louisa Bingley Hurst
Hurst – Mr. Hurst
Charles Bingley – Charles Bingley
Caroline Bingley – Caroline Bingley

"JC" Collins – Mr. Collins
Charlotte Lucas – Charlotte Lucas
Wickham – George Wickham

Sense and Sensibility

The Dashwoods
Mrs. Du – Mrs. Dashwood
Alice Du – Elinor Dashwood
Vivian Du – Marianne Dashwood
Amy Du – Margaret Dashwood

Mrs. Jennings – Mrs. Jennings
Peter Feng – Edward Ferrars
Lucy Ying – Lucy Steele
Niall Brandon – Colonel Brandon
Austen Willoughby – John Willoughby

ACKNOWLEDGMENTS

Confession: I love reading acknowledgments. I always skip ahead and read them before I finish a book—usually before I even finish the first chapter. It's the one place in a book that you can actually get to know an author instead of her characters. I've waited a long time to write my own.

First, I'm grateful for my Heavenly Father and His Son. The Atonement is the only thing that makes it possible for me to improve as a writer and a person. I am grateful They have a plan for my life that's always so much better than the plans I come up with myself.

To my family, thanks for being so cool. I love us when we all get together, and I love each of you individually too: Dad, Mom, James and Alecia, Jenny, Rob, Kaeli and Sam, Ali, Tom, and now the next generation—Tyler and Leona.

Thanks to Nana and Gramps too for all your love and for inspiring me to live up to the Doxey name. And thanks to the rest of my extended family for the hugs and support and questions about what I'm writing next.

To each of my friends, thank you—thank you for being the awesome people that you are. Not to turn this into one of those lame Facebook posts, but I seriously have the coolest people in my life. I wish I could name you all, but no one wants to read acknowledgments that are that long. Not even me.

Of course, there are a few friends I need to thank specifically. Big thanks to Jess Kartchner for owning the couch on which I wrote the first draft of this book. And to Lizz Wu for owning the super cute house in which that couch still resides. I love you guys. Thanks, Jacob and Chris for driving me to Berkeley all those times—pretty sure you're the reason this book is set in Kensington. Thanks to Arie, Aubrey, Brody, Christy, Jen, Jess Deal, Jess Hunter, Josie, Kimiko, Liz, Nani, Nick, and everyone else who read my writing before it was worth publishing and graciously flattered me into the idea that I could do this.

One of the best things about working for your publisher is that you get to spend lots of time with the awesome folks who do all the behind-the-scenes work to make your dreams come true. (And, when it comes time to write your acknowledgments, you know all their names.)

Thanks to Bryce, Lyle, and Lee for making this all possible.

Thanks to Emma for lots of emails with the word "yay!" in them. Thanks to Melissa, my one-time desk buddy, for out-editing me. Thanks to Michelle for taking my crazy cover ideas and turning them into something amazing. And thanks to Kelly for convincing me to start a blog and pushing me to be a real author.

Also mucho mucho thanks to Emily, Hannah B., Lynnae, and Emmett for overall awesomeness; Shawnda, Jessica, and Kevin for taking care of me when I'm not writing fiction; Sydnee, Rebecca, Angela, and Jim for being way more technologically savvy than I'll ever be and doing favors for me so I don't lose my mind; to Eileen, Lauren, and Jen for being so fun to visit that it's worth the trip downstairs; to Justin for knowing everything, even if it drives me bonkers, and Shaun for being willing to do whatever I ask; to Angie, Donna, and Claire for making it so that I actually look forward to Tuesday meetings; to Lauren for calling me "Hildy" and Lexie for the time she bought me Chipotle; to Bevan for making me laugh and Hannah P. for answering all my questions; to Kat, Cindy, Glen, Hersshy, Spencer, Scott, Laurie, and everyone else—I'm so grateful for all that you do for me as Author Heidi and just Regular Heidi. And a special thanks to Heather for always cheering me on and to Deborah for making me laugh every day.

There. Don't you feel like you know me so much better now?

But wait, we're not done yet. Because the most important people I need to thank are you guys. Thanks to everyone who read this book! (Or if you're like me and you skipped ahead to read the acknowledgments page, thanks to everyone who is currently reading chapter one of this book.) You are amazing. How do I know? I just do. It's one of those author superpowers.

I love you all!

Finally, of course, thanks to Jane Austen. And . . . uh . . . sorry. About all this. If it's any consolation, you're welcome to borrow the fictional people I've come up with and write your own story about them. Only I doubt you'd want to. Your characters are way cooler.

ABOUT THE AUTHOR

Heidi Jo Doxey has been reading Jane Austen's novels over and over and over again since middle school—long before she ever dreamed of writing a book herself.

She lives in Utah, where she works in publishing, but she still calls the San Francisco Bay Area home. When she's not writing or reading, she enjoys hiking, riding her bike, playing volleyball, traveling, watching movies, and spending time with family and friends.

Visit her online at girlwiththeanswers.blogspot.com or JaneJournals.com.

0
26575
16829
7